KNASIM
A RICHMOND CRIME FAMILY SAGA

TACARRA

Doing what you were born to do should be a simple task, right? That's how Knasim felt when it came time for him to become the heir to The Richmond Crime Family aka The RCF. Yet, he is being thrusted into an arranged marriage, something he doesn't feel he needs to do to run an empire. Yet, Knasim remains loyal to his father and is ready to fulfill his duty. Only when he meets his "future wife", she's not who he wants... he wants someone else, someone who will also allow him to fulfill his duty.

Controlling the streets is one thing Knasim knows how to do, but will his efforts to control the fate of his personal life interfere with his ability to do his job? And can everyone involved come out on top, with feelings, egos, and hearts intact? Knasim realizes that there's more to being at the top than just being at the top. He better pray he has what it takes to stay there, or the snakes will slither out of the grass, ready to test anything that seems like a weakness.

KNASIM One

"Damn. Y'all ain't finished unpacking them niggas yet? It looks like a fuckin' morgue in this bitch." I turned to my brother Knight to see if he was serious. The look on his face told me he was.

"Nigga, you do know this shit is a morgue, right? The fuck else it's supposed to look like?" Sometimes I wondered about this nigga. Shit never made sense, but in his world, it did. My family is the founders of Richmond Crime Family. We had our hands in a little bit of everything here in Wood Haven or The Wood, as we like to refer it to. The Wood was composed of five sections. The Heights were the projects or the hood if you preferred that term. That's where shit got real grimy and muthafuckas didn't give a fuck about shit over there. The Estates and The Hills were where the upper echelon lived...my family included. The Valley was where the middle class resided, and The Bay was just that...the bay. It was near the water. That's where I lived. Shit was peaceful as fuck out there, and I needed that after dealing with shit like this all day.

We had funeral homes all over The Wood, but the one

where we did most of our shit was located in The Valley. Each home served a different purpose. The one that we were at now was the one that we got our shipment of pills. The bodies would come through The Bay and were sent off to their prospective houses. Our cousins, Kyandri and Kyan, kept their guns out at that house. The Estates and The Hills were where the coke and heroin were kept, and The Heights was where we kept the weed. Shit ran smoothly and efficiently.

"I know what the fuck it is. What I don't know is why these bodies not in the fuckin' incinerator? Y'all in here doing some funny shit with these corpses?" He stared at the workers, who were a mixture of women and men, with a look of repulsion on his face.

"Aye, go find something to do. I'll handle this." That nigga's patience was too short. I tried to be level-headed at all times, but that didn't always work out in my favor, especially if my brother was around. I didn't have time to deal with his shit right now. Our pops was already on my fuckin' nerves. Every move I made, he had to go behind me like I was some damn little kid. I wish he would sit his old ass down somewhere. After I got Knight's unstable ass out of the room, I checked to make sure that everything was accounted for. Everything looked to be in place. After giving my orders to the workers, I went to go find my brother. When I got up front, he was outside sitting in the car, rolling a blunt.

"You finished babysitting them muthafuckas?" he asked once I approached my all black Escalade.

"Am I finished doing your fuckin' job? Yeah, I am." I got in and started the engine and waited for this fool to finish rolling his blunt. I didn't smoke, but I wasn't against those who did.

My brother being the main one. He was finally finished, and I was able to pull off.

"Man, it's only Monday and I'm already over this shit. I hate this time of the fuckin' month," he fussed, lighting the tip of his blunt and taking a deep pull.

"You don't say that shit when it's time to collect so shut all that damn whining up. You sound like a bitch," I poked.

"I got yo' bitch. You just worry about Knox and the bullshit he got you on. That's the only bitch you need to worry about." I glanced over at him, and he had a stupid ass smirk on his face that I wanted to knock down his fuckin' throat. He thought the shit was funny that Knox, our pops, was trying to get me to marry some bitch I didn't know. He knew I wasn't with the shit but insisted, since we would form a partnership with the girl's family. Fuck that bitch and her family. We didn't need them for shit, and he knew that. He just hated to relinquish control so invoking this dumb ass arranged marriage rule is his way of maintaining some source of power. Even though I was next in line to head the family, I didn't want to go along with this shit. How the fuck was I expected to marry a girl I didn't even know? The fuck they do that at? I guess The Wood would be the first, but if I can help the shit, it wouldn't be happening at all.

"You let me worry about Knox, and you worry about Teyana's looney ass." That got his ass to shut up. Teyana was his bat shit crazy ex that tried to kill his ass at least once a week. They were dysfunctional as fuck, but I guess he loved that shit.

"Ain't nobody studdin' Tey's ass. She'll be the fuck alright. I told her I was off her, but she don't seem to comprehend that shit."

"I guess not if you keep fuckin' on her. What do you expect?"

"I expect her to know that I just wanna fuck and that's it. Ain't my problem she don't know the difference," he shrugged like it was nothing. I didn't even respond to his dumb ass logic because in his head...it made sense.

"Yeah, let me get you out of my shit. I got other shit to do besides chauffer you around. You got more than one vehicle, yet you find yourself in my passenger seat."

"You worrying about the wrong shit. All you need to be concerned with is that you did your big brother duties for today. Not my shit." I stared at this fool while I pulled through his gate and up the driveway. I didn't have time to do this. I've been gone all day, and I was tired as fuck.

"Get out," I stated. I didn't even bother to put my shit in park because I was pulling off as soon as he got his ass out.

"Damn, nigga. Let me collect my shit first. Fuck!" he groaned. I looked in the rearview mirror and saw Teyana pull behind me. She must've had a tracking device on this nigga's nuts or some shit.

"Aye, tell Tey to move that shit before I run over it. I know she sees my damn brake lights, so why would she do that dumb shit?" I was tired and fuckin' annoyed. Playing with this ditzy ass girl was not on my to-do list. "Why didn't you remove the sensor from her car so she couldn't get through the gate?"

"Man, I forgot. Let me get this foolish girl from my shit. I'll holla at you in the morning." He stuck his hand out, and we slapped each other's hand twice before he shut the door.

"Man, Tey! Move yo' shit, bruh. Why would you park behind him like that?" I heard Knight fussing. Her ass jumped out of the car and still didn't move her shit. See, she was trying to piss me off, but I had a trick for that. I let up off the brake and let my shit roll back into the front of her car and backed her shit into the gate and out into the street.

"Knas! What the fuck is wrong with you? Knight, are you just going to let him push my car out the way like that?" she yelled. I heard them going back and forth, but that didn't have shit to do with me. I told his ass I was tired and wasn't about to play these damn games with them. I was taking my ass home and go to bed. I had to do this shit all over again in the morning.

———

Knight wanted me to meet his ass at our cousin's Kyan's club tonight. He and his twin brother Kyandri were my uncle Kenton's son's. They ran his faction of The RCF since he was dead. Kyandri or Trig, as we called him. Shit was short for Trigga because that nigga's trigger stayed ready and didn't discriminate. He was over the gun distribution while his brother was the hitta for The RCF. Nobody knew what that nigga did besides run this club and the adjoining hotel and casino, and it was best that way. Anyway, I didn't have shit else planned, so here I was, ready to unwind. Making my way inside, I headed straight to our reserved VIP section, where I knew my brother and cousins were waiting for me with a few bottles and a few bitches to go along with them. When I got to the top, I saw the party was in full effect already.

"Wassup up, bruh?" Knight greeted me with our handshake and a head nod.

"Nigga, do you always have to look like you just leaving a photoshoot for GQ Magazine?" I slapped hands with Trig before doing the same to his brother.

"You sound like a hating ass nigga. Don't hate on it, my boy. The ladies love this shit." he smirked.

"Yeah, and Denver gon' love beating yo' ass."

"Denver ain't gon' do shit," he waved off. We all laughed because we knew that was a lie.

"What's good, cuz. It's been a minute since you fell through. You good?" Murda asked.

"Ain't shit been going on besides your uncle getting on my fuckin' nerves." I don't know why he won't get off my back about this shit. I don't need to be married to run a fuckin' business. Shit, really pissing me the fuck off. Every day, he brought this shit up, and every day I told him I ain't wit' the shit.

"He still on that marriage shit?" he asked.

"Hell yeah. He's really pissing me the fuck off, too."

"You know how Knox is. He thinks he's that old nigga, Victor Newman, or some shit. I let the nigga do whatever the fuck he wants so he can leave me the fuck alone," Knight inputted.

"Yeah, I'm not doing all that. How the fuck is he going to tell me who the fuck to marry? Where they do that at? This ain't no fuckin' soap opera." I was getting angry all over again, thinking about how he was trying to control my life. Since I was the oldest, he always put the most pressure on me to lead by example and follow in his footsteps. I did, to a certain extent, but I had to draw the line somewhere.

"I'm glad my pops was younger and didn't think of any shit like that," Trig mentioned. He was a year older than me, but I guess when my grandfather first organized The RCF, he made it to where it always went to the oldest son of the oldest son. That's probably where my pops got the shit from because he really thought he was a King 'round this bitch.

"I wish it did apply to yo' ass. At least you already got a girl, and the shit would be simpler."

"Look. Let's turn the fuck up tonight and worry about that other shit later. It's plenty of girls in here that you can choose from. Don't let Pops fuck up all that." He was right. I came to enjoy my night, and that's exactly what I planned on doing. We ordered two more bottles of Hennessy Black. Niggas wasted their money buying expensive shit trying to show off money they know they didn't have for that nasty high priced shit. You can't go wrong with Hennessy. That was my shit, so I was sticking to it. Just as the bottle girl sauntered off, I spotted a chick walking across the way with her friends in tow. She was a sexy chocolate thing that I could see myself ending my night with. She didn't look familiar, and that was a good thing. She must've felt someone looking at her because her eyes met mine and she smirked.

Oh, she's a bold one.

I tapped my brother on the shoulder and directed his attention towards the other section.

"Aye, check this shit out. Chocolate shorty in the next section, over."

"Damn," he huffed. "I hate you saw her first, but do what you do." I dapped my brother up and nodded for ol' girl to come over and join us. She came over with her three friends following closely behind and she sat her eager ass right next to me.

"I was wondering what took you so long to invite me over. I've had my eyes on you since I've walked in." Her accent was sexy as fuck. I don't know what it was, and I really didn't give a fuck. She was just what I needed to end my night and rid myself of today's bullshit.

Leaning back, throwing back my shot, I finally let her know what my plan was. "Look, shorty. All I want to do is fuck. I don't even care to know your name or see you after that." Looking her over, I was waiting for her response. If she took too long, I'd gladly take one of her homegirls.

"Shit. Let's go," she declared.

"Aye, bruh. I'm out." I dapped my brother and cousins up and left with shorty walking extremely close to me. When we got outside, she gawked at my ride.

"This all you?" She quizzed.

I just copped the new 2023 Lamborghini Huracan EVO in all white with white, black and chrome interior. With chrome rims, my bitch was definitely bad.

"Yeah. This all me. Get in." I didn't even bother to open the door for her. She didn't know my name, yet she was willing to leave with me and get fucked. What if I were a serial killer or some shit? That lets you know hoes didn't give a fuck as long as there was dick to get out of the situation.

She told me she had a room at my cousin's hotel, *The Royale,* and that was even better. I didn't have to worry about paying for shit, and I could dip out when I got done. Had she told me that sooner, I could've just walked over there, but she didn't need to know I had that kind of access. We got to the hotel, and I parked on the side since she said her room was closer to this side. As soon as we got off of the elevator, shorty dropped to her knees and swallowed my dick like I was about to pay for this pussy.

I threw my head back and bit my lip, enjoying the feeling of her wet mouth and deep throat. She made that shit nasty and sloppy just like a freak bitch would and I was on the verge of cumming down her throat, but I wanted to save that shit until after I sampled the pussy. I tapped the back of her head to let her know to get up.

"Bend over the sofa." I ordered.

"We can go inside my room," she suggested.

"Nah. Bend over." I wasn't about to be doing all that. I just needed to nut so I could go home and go the fuck to sleep.

Taking a condom out of my pocket, I covered my dick and plunged deep inside of her mediocre ass pussy. I should've known this shit would end up like this, but I'm here now, so it is what it is. After ten minutes of her screaming like I was killing her, knowing damn well she wasn't feeling this shit. I wasn't no lil' dick nigga, but shorty's pussy was deeper than the Grand Canyon.

"Aye, get up and come suck this shit out." I was over this shit.

Snatching the condom off, she took me back into her mouth and started back slurping me up just as nasty as the first time. Before I knew it, I was shooting my seeds down her hollow throat. I didn't even waste time with talking. Before I picked up the used condom from the floor, I tucked my dick and pulled my pants back up. I kept some tissue in my pocket just for situations like this. Even though I didn't nut in it, I still didn't trust a bitch not to pull one.

"You're leaving before we get in another round?" she asked, like she knew her pussy was worth the time.

"Yeah. I'm good now." I strolled my ass right on out the door and headed home. I was still frustrated as fuck, but at least she took the edge off.

———

The next morning, my pops had me in his office talking about the same shit...again.

"Knasim! Did you hear anything I said to you?

"Nah, I didn't."

"I said that you need to make an attempt to meet Precious and get to know her. You've put it off long enough and I won't allow you to do it any longer."

I peered at my father like he had gone crazy. The fuck did he mean?

"The fuck you mean, allow me? Pops, I'm grown as fuck, and I don't need you to allow me to do shit! I don't want to meet that damn girl. She might be ugly as hell for all I know. What do I look like messing with an ugly bitch? Let alone marry her?" I slumped down further into my seat because he was feeding me straight bullshit.

"Knasim, rules are rules, son," he tried reasoning.

"Pops, you make the fuckin' rules!"

"And that's to give you some structure! You need to learn some responsibility, so when the time comes, you'll be able to handle business correctly." I sat up when he said that because what the fuck did he mean by correctly?

"You got a problem with the way I do shit, Pops? I mean, I

thought I was already running this shit, but you keep fuckin' forgetting that!" I was over him and this bullshit ass conversation.

"You need a wife, Knasim, to help you with your status. People will be more receptacle of a family man. Not somebody who runs from woman to woman. Marriage shows commitment and structure," he tried reasoning, but I still wasn't hearing the shit, so I got up and walked out. Leaving him looking dumb.

"Her family is flying in sometime this week. Get yourself together before then." I didn't even respond. I left his office and went to search for my mama. She needed to get her husband off my fucking back. I found her in the kitchen with my sister, Knicole.

"'Sup, Knic (Nik)?" I mushed my sister's head before making my way to my mama, kissing her cheek. "Hey, Beautiful."

"Hey baby? You're about to leave already?"

"Yeah. Your husband is getting on my nerves with his bull... mess. Can you get him off my back, please?" I tried using my charm with her like I normally did, but it wasn't working.

"Sweetie, it won't be that bad. Let's just meet the young lady and we can go from there. Okay?"

"You should be lucky somebody's willing to marry your ignorant ass," my sister voiced.

"Knicole! Watch your mouth!" my mother chastised.

"Girl, shut yo' ass up! Sorry, Ma." She cut her eyes at me when I cursed. "I'm about to go. I don't feel the love like I should from here." I kissed my mama on the forehead and hugged my sister. Just as I was headed to the front door, my father appeared.

"Saturday, Knasim." He left it at that and went upstairs.

This bitch better not be ugly. I thought as I got in my car and pulled off.

PROMISE *Two*

We had been in Wood Haven for three days, and I was ready to go. I don't know why my family made me come, anyway. Precious was the one that they were pawning off...not me. My father gave me this big speech about representing a united front. Whatever that meant. All I knew was that I was ready to go home. I was in my room at the house my parents had while we were here. Precious stayed at a hotel for the first few days because she was hanging out with her friends that she brought with her. She was big on partying and being 'outside', and she knew I wasn't on that type of time. Not with her, anyway. I brought some of my supplies with me so I could work on some creams while I was here. I probably could make a few bucks and gain some clientele. I made a different array of skincare items. I had body creams, oils, scrubs, and serums. I even had a haircare line. My products were for men, women, and children. *I-Promise* had a lil' something for everybody. I was in the middle of getting started with my night routine when there was a knock on my room door.

"Come in," I called out. I looked up and my father emerged through the door.

"Hey, Tootsie," my father came in, calling me by the nickname he'd given me as a little because of my love for Tootsie rolls. "Your mama is almost finished with dinner. Why are you up here by yourself?" he asked, taking a seat in the vacant chair that sat by my bed.

"Because I'm ready to go home. I don't know why I had to come, anyway. This is Precious' new family...not mine."

"We'll all be family. Their entire family will be in attendance as well. Besides, we need you to set the tone because you know your sister can be a bit extreme," he chuckled and shook his head. He didn't tell one lie, though. Precious was loose as a goose and she didn't care who knew. I can't even fathom the thought of her being someone's wife.

"Don't I know," I sighed dejectedly. "I'll be down in a few." My father kissed my forehead and left me alone in my room. I stood up and admired myself in the full-length mirror that I had placed on the wall. I loved my chocolate skin, but that wasn't always the case. When I was younger, I had eczema real bad and got teased about it a lot. The steroid creams that the doctors prescribed were too strong and literally burned my skin. So imagine going through middle school, experiencing puberty, and having atrocious skin. I cried so much that I begged my parents to take me out of school. When I got to the point where I wanted to kill myself, that's when they finally gave in. I was removed from school during my seventh-grade year. During that time, I did research on different remedies and ingredients that would help my skin. I went through the trial-and-error stage, and, by my freshman year, I was able to go back to school. Nobody could believe it was me because I was no longer the ugly duckling. I still didn't talk to too many people. Only my friend was Kim. She was the only one that still talked to me when everyone else made fun of me. Now, my skin is clear. My hair was healthy, and my curves had finally come in, but I still felt like an ugly duckling. My sister Precious got all the attention from boys. Most people say it's because she's easy, but she really gorgeous and she knows it. I wish I had her confidence, but at twenty-four, if it hadn't come by now...I could just hang it up.

I finally made it downstairs, and my parents, along with my sister, were already sitting at the table. They looked as if they were waiting for me, so I hurried to my seat.

"Sorry about that. I had to freshen up."

"It's okay. We all just sat down," my mother said. I looked at the spread and rolled my eyes. My father had a heart attack two years ago and ever since then, we ate everything broiled or baked. I was over it. Why did we all have to suffer?

"You need to get out of that room and in these streets. Wood Haven has a lot to offer and you're missing out," Precious commented.

"I'm good. I'm pretty sure you'll explore enough for the both of us," I countered.

"What does that mean?"

"Just what I said."

"Girls!" my father spoke. "Cut it out. I don't know why y'all two argue all the time like you're not sisters. Precious, leave your sister alone and focus on the task at hand. You don't need to be 'out in these streets' when you came here to meet the man you're supposed to marry. How do you think that'll look?"

"Daddy, all I'm doing is having fun. Me and my friends only went to a few clubs and bars. I'm not entertaining anybody, knowing I'm about to meet my dream man." I rolled my eyes inward at her comment because I knew it was a bunch a bullshit.

"Well, I hope you're ready for Saturday. We're meeting with the family then and going over details. Do you have a list of things that you might want to ask for?" he asked.

"Sure do." She wore a smirk on her face, and I knew that meant she was up to no good.

For the rest of dinner, I tuned everybody out. I didn't care to indulge in that conversation. Whatever they had going on with this Richmond family didn't have anything to do with me, and I didn't care.

————

I finally decided to go out and see that this city had to offer. It was so pretty out here, and the palm trees were to die for. I wanted to see what natural skincare stores they had so I could see if I had some competition. My driver pulled up to the small strip mall. After I told him I would call him when I got ready, he nodded and left. Going inside the first shop, it was filled with a lot of designer clothes and shoes. Even though I had access to my father's money, I wouldn't dare spend it frivolously on clothes. Precious, on the other hand, would've tried to clear their inventory. As I was looking around, a lady walked up to me and offered me a glass of champagne.

"Welcome to *Charme.* If you need anything, don't hesitate to let me know." She walked off and left me to continue to browse the racks. I'd admit, they did have a few pieces I couldn't pass up. They weren't my speed, but Precious would love them. I placed the champagne flute down and admired the mint green dress pressed up against my body. It looked nice, but where would I wear it? I placed one down and placed two more against my body.

"I like the orange one, shorty. That shit looked sexy against your pretty chocolate skin." I jumped at the sound of a man behind me. When I turned around, I had to be tripping. There's no way that this fine ass specimen was talking to me. Before me stood the finest man God had ever put his hands on. He looked well over six feet and had skin that looked as chocolate and smooth as mine. He had a mass of kinky coils on the top of his head that were tapered on the sides, connecting to a full, thick beard that surrounded the prettiest lips I've ever seen on a man. I started looking around to make sure I wasn't going crazy.

"You're talking to me?" I asked incredulously.

"Nobody over here but you, baby girl." His deep voice flowed to places that they had no business. I had to quickly find my words, or I'd just be standing here looking like a fool.

"Thank you." He nodded before walking off.

I hope this town wasn't too big where I wouldn't run into him again.

I took the pieces that I decided on to the counter and the lady started bagging up everything for me. When she was done, she handed the bag to me, before telling me to have a nice day.

"Wait...I didn't pay for this."

"The gentleman before you put it on his tab." She smiled. I

looked around the store and towards the door, but he was nowhere in sight.

"Uhh...thank you. If he comes back, can you tell him I said thank you?" She nodded, and I headed out the door. After I went to a few more shops, I finally got ready to call my driver.

"Did you get the dress?" I heard behind me again. When I turned around, the handsome stranger was once again in my presence.

"I did. Thank you. You didn't have to do that, but my granny always told me never to look a gift horse in the mouth. It'll block my blessings and I definitely don't want to do that," I revealed.

"Sounds like your granny was a smart woman." I nodded. My driver pulled up just in time because we were just standing there in an awkward silence.

"Thank you again..." I paused because I didn't know his name.

"...Knas," he rendered.

"Thank you, Knas." I rushed off to my ride before he could say anything else. Once I was inside, I released the breath that I was holding and rested my head on the seat.

"Maybe this move wouldn't be so bad after all," I thought as I got lost in my thoughts.

KNASIM Three

It was finally Saturday, and I was getting ready to go to my parent's house for this fuck ass dinner I didn't want to be a part of in the first place. I didn't care what he said, I wasn't marrying a bitch I didn't know just so he could call himself teaching me a lesson. I was single, so I was going to do single shit. When the time came, I would know how to adjust and act accordingly. It was all bullshit to me. While I was dressing, my phone went off, and it was Knight.

"Yeah?" I answered.

"You got Pops over here 'bout to blow his shit. Why you ain't here yet?"

"He'll be alright, and I'll get there when I get there. I ain't ask for this shit," I grumbled.

"Hurry up and get yo' ass here, nigga. You damn sure gon' be in for some shit." He hung up, and I finished getting dressed.

Finally finished getting dressed, I grabbed my keys and headed out. I was purposely late just to piss my old man off. He wanted this shit, not me.

Pulling up to my parent's house, I noticed another vehicle

that didn't belong to my brother or sister. I let myself in and followed the voices that were coming from the family room. I stepped inside and my pops and brother were sitting down talking to some strange nigga. He must've been the girl's father.

"Here's the betrothed groom now," my father announced.

"The what?" I quizzed, looking at him skeptically. Out of the corner of my eye, I saw Knight smirking.

"Son, this is Thaddeus. Your future father-in-law. Thad, this is my oldest son, Knasim." Pops made his introductions like I really cared about this nigga or his daughter.

"'Sup." I threw a head nod and sat in the empty chair.

"So, Knasim. Precious is excited about meeting you."

"I bet she is," I muttered as my mother came to tell us that dinner was ready.

Everyone followed her into the dining room and just as I rounded the corner, I bumped into a soft body.

"Oh, excuse me. I'm sorry. I wasn't paying attention." I looked down and saw the girl from the boutique. If she was who I was marrying, then I might reconsider this lil' situation after all. There was this innocent aura about her that couldn't be missed.

"You're good, shorty. Accidents happen." I smirked, and she blushed at my statement. Knight still had that dumb ass look on his face like he was retarded or some shit. I followed shorty around the corner and as soon as I entered the dining room, I just knew my eyes were playing tricks on me.

"Yo, what the fuck are you doing here? You following me or some shit?" I snapped at ol' girl I left the club with the other night.

"Knasim!" My father's voice boomed.

"What's going on here?" Thaddeus quizzed, looking at his whore ass daughter.

"Knasim. Do you know Precious?" My mother asked.

"Nah, I don't. If she's who y'all trying to get me to wife, you can cancel that shit. This damn girl just learned my name but had my dick down her throat the other night." You could hear gasps from everyone in the room, but I didn't give a fuck.

"Oh, shit!" Knight instigated. He knew exactly who she was because he saw her the night at the club.

"Knight!" my mother chastised.

"Precious! Is this true?" The woman who I assumed was her mother asked.

"He didn't ask my name, and I didn't ask his. It's not like it's a bad thing. We already know what to expect now." She shrugged.

"Y'all must be crazy as hell if you think I'm about to marry somebody that let a nigga bang her without even knowing his name. Pops, I don't know what y'all take me for but this ain't it." I was getting ready to leave when my father stopped me.

"Knasim, come with me." I stared at him for a few moments before I followed him back to his office. As soon as we were inside, I went in.

"Pops, I'm not marrying that fuckin' girl. I knew this shit was a bad idea. I just fucked that girl a few nights ago without even knowing her damn name and vice versa and you expect me to marry her? Be for real, Pops." Sighing heavily, my father looked at me sympathetically.

"Son, I know how it looks, but we need this merger."

"We don't need shit. You're just trying to dictate my life and I'm not going for it. This is bullshit, Pops, and you know it."

We were in a stare off for a few seconds before he spoke again.

"Look, you need to make up your mind. I know it's not orthodox but trust me, son. It'll be for the better of both families if you do this." I heard my father and really didn't give a fuck. He could say whatever the fuck he wanted. I wasn't doing shit. I turned to leave and heard him sigh. At that moment I came up with something.

"Look, I'll think about doing this shit, but it'll be my way and on my terms, or I'm not doing it at all." He looked at me for a moment before nodding. We headed back into the dining room and everybody's eyes were on me.

"Look, Knasim. I apologize for my daughter's brash behavior. What she did was shameful and definitely not the actions of a wife. If you need more time to think about this or have her go to counseling, we understand," Thaddeus spoke, but it was unnecessary.

"Nah, ain't none of that necessary. We're both grown and did what we wanted, but like I told my pops, if I agree to this shit, it'll be on my terms." I looked him straight in the eye to let him know I meant what the fuck I said.

"Go ahead. I'm willing to compromise for the humiliation."

"If I agree to this situation, I won't be marrying Precious' hoe ass." I heard her kiss her teeth, but I didn't give a fuck. "I want her," I revealed, looking at the girl I bumped into earlier.

"What?" both girls shrieked at the same time.

"Those are my conditions. If you can't get with it, fine by me. I just know it won't be her." I pointed at Precious.

At this point, I really didn't care what they decided. I meant what I said. I wasn't marrying no fucking hoe. If I couldn't have the other one, then Pops would have to come up with another plan because I was standing on what I said.

"Wait...let's talk. The deal was with Precious...not Promise," her father said. It didn't matter because my mind was already made up.

"The deal was that I was to marry your daughter. You have two, so I don't see what the problem is."

"Look, everybody, let's just sit down and eat so we can work all this out. I'm pretty sure we can come up with a sensible solution," my mother recommended.

"Nah, Ma. I'm out. Y'all figure this shit out."

I left out the same way I came in. If they wanted me to do this shit, then they'd do it my way or get the fuck on out of my face.

I was still stuck in the same spot I was in when I heard Knasim's request. There was no way I was hearing him right. I was not marrying his ass. I didn't come here for this, so I hope they knew better than to go along with that bullshit. All eyes were on me, and I wish they'd focus their attention on something else other than me.

"Uhm, Knox. I apologize for all of this. Let me go home and talk to my family and I'll get back to you," my father said. There was nothing to talk about, so I don't know why he was sitting here lying to this man.

"That's fine, Thad. It'll give us some time to talk to Knasim as well. I apologize for his behavior as well. We'll be in touch." Mr. Richmond escorted our family to the door, and we all piled inside the of the truck and waited for our father to pull off. The truck wasn't even in gear good before my father went in on Precious.

"Precious, what the fuck is wrong with you? Out of all places, why would you come to this city displaying that kind of behavior? You knew what we were coming here for and how important this merger was for us! Do you have a better way for us to conduct business, because clearly selling your box is out of the question because he didn't seem impressed at all."

"Thaddeus! That's enough! We'll continue this conversation at home," my mother spoke. She rarely intervened when my father was talking, but he was being a bit extreme. Even I felt a lil' bad for Precious.

The rest of the ride was quiet. It was about a thirty-minute drive from the Richmond Estate to ours. When the truck came to a stop, Precious wasted no time getting out. I followed behind her with my parent's following suit. Once we were in the house, all hell broke loose.

"You happy now?" she turned and asked me. I had to look around to see who she was talking to because clearly it wasn't me.

"You're talking to me?" I asked, pointing at my chest.

"Yeah, I'm talking to you. You always thought you were better than me and you had to go and flirt with him, knowing he was supposed to be with me!" she yelled.

"You can't be serious right now? I haven't seen that man a day before yesterday and—"

"Wait. You saw him yesterday?" my father cut me off.

"Yes. I ran into him at the boutique I went to. He introduced himself and paid for my things without my knowledge," I explained.

"Oh, so he's trickin' off on you?" Precious commented.

"That's enough, Precious!" my mother chastised, causing Precious to roll her eyes.

"How was I supposed to know who he was? It's not like we knew any names or faces. He told me his name was Knas.

That's it. My meeting him by chance is no different from Precious meeting him."

"Did you sleep with him?" my father asked.

"No!" I rushed out. I couldn't believe he asked me something like that.

"He's just saying he wants her just to make me jealous. I already had him anyway, so it's whatever," she shrugged.

"Precious, just be quiet. We wouldn't even be in this predicament if you knew how to act like you had some sense, some fuckin' time! I thought a husband would be able to get you under control, because God knows you dodged every one of me and your mother's attempts." My father looked disappointed, and that made my heart break. I wanted to beat Precious' ass for always doing dumb shit. I didn't quite know what my father did for a living, but I knew it had to be illegal. I never saw him clock in at nobody's job, but he always provided us with the finer things. Whatever the Richmond's were offering, he must've really needed it.

"Look, everybody's emotions are all over the place. Let's get some rest and we'll continue this conversation in the morning." My mother spoke while Precious rolled her eyes and stomped off like a spoiled brat. I was still standing stuck in the same spot before my father came over and kissed my forehead before he left me still in the same spot.

I went upstairs and into my room so that I could shower and forget all of this shit that happened because right now; I felt like I was in the Twilight Zone. After doing my face routine, I got in the shower and used my shea butter and jojoba oil body wash. It had a hint of papaya extract to add a soft tropical scent. This had to be one of my favorites. Once I got out of the shower, I oiled my body with my signature oil and dressed for bed. Before I went to sleep, I had to call Kim and tell her about this shit.

"Hey girl. I was just about to text you and see what you were up to. Y'all back from dinner already?" she rambled off.

"Girl. Let me tell you about that ghetto ass shit. You remember the dude I texted you about yesterday?"

"Yeah," she dragged out.

"Well, why he was the dude Precious was supposed to marry?"

"Bitch, you lying!"

"That ain't all. How about they fucked a few days ago and neither one of them knew who the other one was."

"Damn. We'll at least they both know what they're getting into."

"You would think. He wasn't having that, though. He flat out told my daddy that he wasn't marrying no hoe," I giggled.

"I know you lying! What did Precious say?"

"What could she say? It wasn't like he was lying. But, Kim. Listen, when I tell you this. You ready?" I was nervous, like he was standing right here looking at me.

"What, bitch? Damn. I'on have time to play twenty-questions with you. What happened?"

"He said he wasn't marrying Precious and the only way he would go through with whatever deal our fathers have, he had to marry me," I blurted out in one damn breath.

Silence.

"Kim?"

"I'm here. I'm just stuck because I didn't expect yo' ass to say that. The fuck, Promise? Are you serious? Is he serious?"

"Apparently, so," I sighed.

"What did your parents say? she asked.

"That we'll talk about it tomorrow. I don't know what there is to talk about. Precious was their pawn in this lil' game. Not me."

"I mean...you did say he was fine," Kim voiced.

"And? That doesn't mean I wanted to marry the nigga. Plus, he had sex with my sister. How fuckin' weird and gross is that?" I scrunched my face up just at the thought.

"Clearly it wasn't enough to lock his ass down," she joked, causing me to laugh right along with her.

"Look, I'm not doing all of that. They can figure it out without me. I don't know that man other than his name. How in the hell can he be my husband? He better dust Precious' ass off and try again."

I continued my conversation with Kim for another hour, catching up on things back home. I was going to see if she could come down here with me because if we were staying longer, I might need her company. I didn't make friends easily, and I wasn't about to try so that I could set myself up to look stupid. After saying my goodbyes to Kim, I plugged my phone up and got under the covers. I hope my parents had their minds right in the morning.

———

A few days had passed since the whole debacle at the Richmond's. I tried to avoid my father at all costs, but I didn't have much luck today. While I was handling my hygiene, he came to my bedroom door and told me to meet him downstairs. I knew I couldn't avoid him forever. Precious hadn't been here since that night. I don't know if she went back home to Cannon Hills or not. Knowing her, she was out doing the exact same thing that got me in this predicament to begin with. After finishing my face routine, I dressed in a t-shit and leggings. It was raining, and I had no plans to leave the house today. When I got down there, my father was sitting with my mother and Mr. Richmond. I already didn't like the look of us.

"Daddy, what's this?" I asked as I took a seat in the empty chair opposite of our guest.

"Sweetheart, we wanted to talk to you about your arrangement. It's been a few days and time is winding down. We need to continue with business, and this arrangement is vital to our business," my father explained.

"What business is that, exactly?" He kept saying he needed this merger for business, but what business was it?

"Look, sweetheart. Your father needs my business to continue with his. I usually don't offer my services to outsiders, but I made an exception because of the situation at hand. Your father's partner could no longer fulfill his obligations, so he's having to take another route. In return for me helping him, he's doing me a favor in return. My son, Knasim, needs a family structure to calm him down. A wife will do that for him. If he has someone that he has to answer to, then he'll be able to handle the pressure of things when business gets hectic. He needs a balance and right now he doesn't have that." I listened to his father and still wanted to know what all of this has to do with me.

"Again...what does this have to do with me?"

"He already seems to be attracted to you, so the transition may be easy for him."

"And what about me?"

"What do you want?" I wasn't expecting him to ask me that. I didn't know what I wanted because I didn't want to do this shit. I looked around and all eyes were on me. I felt like I was in an interrogation room.

"Give me thirty days to think about it," I responded.

"That's doable, but under one condition." Mr. Richmond was looking directly at me when he spoke, like my parents weren't in the room.

"Use these thirty days as a trial run. Get to know my son, so that the both of you can get acquainted with one another. I know this a lot on you, and I want you to be comfortable as possible. Both of you deserve to know who you're marrying, and I think the trial period will work in everyone's favor." I looked from him to my parents and all three sets of eyes were piercing into me.

"Can I sleep on it?" I asked.

"Sure. You and your family can come for dinner tomorrow night." He stood to leave, prompting my father to stand.

"We'll see you tomorrow, Knox. She'll have her answer ready for you then," my father assured. He shook hands with Mr. Richmond and walked him to the door. When he returned to the living room, he approached me.

"I know you're going to do what's best for the family, Toot-sie. You doing this in place of your sister is very admirable, and I'm beyond appreciative." He kissed me on the top of my head and walked off. I stood in the same spot for a few minutes because I wasn't expecting or prepared for none of this shit.

"It'll be okay, sweetheart. Knasim doesn't seem that bad, and you have a month to get to know him. Use that to your advantage." My mother patted my shoulder and walked off. After standing in the same spot for a few minutes, I headed back to my room.

I didn't come here for this shit.

KHASIM Five

"So, what you gon' do?" I was sitting in my office drinking straight out of the bottle. I may have been attracted to Promise, but that didn't mean I wanted to be married to her ass. Leave it to Knox Richmond to try and force some shit. He inherited everything he had from my grandfather, Knixon. When he got the shit, he wasn't married to my mother. He's really pissing me off with all these so-called rules.

"I don't fuckin' know." I took another swig from the bottle. "He called me talking about we're having another dinner tomorrow to talk over the shit," I huffed.

"Man...I don't know. It might not be that bad. You already said you were feeling shorty."

"That don't mean I want to marry her ass. I don't know shit about that damn girl. She might be crazy as hell for all I know. Wake up in the middle of the night and she just staring in my face and shit." This was bullshit. I was trying to psyche myself that I could make it work off the simple fact that she was fine as hell, but the pretty ones were either crazy or slow and I didn't have time to deal with either.

"Look, I know Knox being on some other shit right now but just hear them out tonight. It might not be that bad after all. At least you won't be stuck with her hoe ass sister," he reasoned.

"You saying all this shit now, but you won't be saying all this shit if he was trying to make you marry Teyana's crazy ass," I countered.

"Bullshit. I don't give a fuck what he was talkin'. I ain't marrying Teyana's ass if she was the last woman that walked the face of the Earth. I'd go snatch up one of them aliens first." I couldn't do nothing but laugh at this fool because I knew he was dead ass serious.

We chopped it up a lil' longer while we waited for the workers to finish up. I'm only here today because we actually had a funeral to prepare for and I needed to meet with the family. This was the only time you'd catch me in a suit. I was more comfortable dressed down. My pops hated that about me and my brother. We'd walk in business meetings in track suits and not give a fuck. He preferred us to dress like our cousin Kyandri. That nigga slept in a suit. It was very rare that you caught him dressed down. Dressed down to him was just a simple dress shirt and slacks. Nigga always looked like he was going somewhere to handle business. Don't let that shit fool you though because he was just as deadly and me and Knight. Especially his twin brother, Kyan. That nigga was fuckin' nuts.

After another hour, I was pulling up to my house and forced myself to get ready for this fuck ass dinner tonight. I was over this shit, but I'd be lying if I said I wasn't low key geeked about seeing Promise's lil' fine ass again tonight. That was the only highlight of this bullshit.

————

I pulled up to my parents' house and exhaled deeply before I turned my car off and got out. I got here early so I could talk to my pops before Promise and her people got here. When I got inside, I found my mama in the kitchen with my sister, Knicole. When they noticed me, Knicole spoke first.

"Well, look at the happy groom," she joked.

"Fuck on wit' that shit, Knic." I scowled at her ass because the shit wasn't funny.

"Watch your mouth, Knasim. You're early," my mother pointed out.

"I needed to talk to Pops before they got here. He in his office?" I asked. She nodded. I walked off and headed to my father's office and walked in. He was looking over some papers that were spread out in front of him. He took his glasses off and sat back and looked at me.

"You're early," he announced.

"I see everybody in this muthafucka knows how to tell time. Didn't you say you wanted to talk about some shit before they got here?" He grimaced before handing me a piece of paper.

"What is this?" I asked, not bothering to read over it.

"It's a contract that states that you will marry Promise and take over as head of The RCF." I looked up from the paper and at my father like he had lost his fuckin' mind.

"You for real right now?"

"As real as it gets. I need assurance that you will do things according to plan," he stated.

Huffing, I looked over the document and stopped at the sentence that stuck out to me.

"Why does this say that I have to be married within ninety days and stay married for a minimum of three years before I gain full control of The RCF? The fuck kind of shit is this, Pops?" I was fucking fuming. This nigga couldn't be for real right now.

"Because those will be the terms between you and The RCF. The three years will give you time to adjust and by then, you'll be thirty and ready."

"So, if you weren't planning to give me complete control until I turned thirty, why the fuck am I doing this?"

"Because it's a business move," he stated flatly.

"Nah, this just another one of your bullshit ass power moves." I slammed the papers back on the desk and stalked out of his office. I ran right into my mother.

"Calm down, son. The Sterling's are here, and you don't want to go out there and they see you like this." She tried calming me down, but that shit wasn't working.

"Ma. I'on give a fu...I'on care how they see me. They just better be lucky if I decide to go through with this bullshit," I huffed. She gave me a look that let me know she wanted to knock my shit loose for cursing. I usually didn't curse in front of my mother unless I was pissed the fuck off, and this was one of those moments.

"Go clean up and get yourself together while I go get your father." She patted my chest and walked around me and headed toward my father's office.

Turning to the corner to get to the nearest bathroom, I collided with a soft body...again.

"Damn, shorty. We got to stop meeting like this." I licked my lips as my eyes scanned over her small frame. This was easily the prettiest girl I have ever seen, but that didn't mean I wanted to be forced into a marriage with her ass.

"Sorry. I need to start paying more attention to where I'm going," she murmured.

I was still extremely close to her ass before she finally tore her eyes from mine and walked away. Going inside the bathroom, I washed my hands and made my way to the dining room where everybody else was. When I got there, I was glad to see that her hoe ass sister wasn't in attendance, but neither was my brother. Knicole sat by Promise, talking her head off like she knew the damn girl. That's what she did, though. She always said she could tell if a person was genuine or not by their energy. I'm going to assume that Promise's energy passed the vibe check. I took the empty seat by to Promise and sat quietly. I needed Knight here to have as a distraction and somebody to talk to, so I took my phone out to text this nigga.

Me: Tf you at nigga?

Lil' Bro: Man...I'll tell you about it later.

I pocketed my phone because I knew whatever the reason had to do with Teyana's ass.

"Knasim, do you have any questions for Promise?" my father asked, further pissing me off. I had been sitting in my seat, eating silently as they held their own conversations.

"Not wit' all y'all looking in my mouth," I retorted. I saw my father's jaw clench, but I gave not one single fuck.

"Knasim," my mother called my name and gave me a warning look. I was over this shit.

Looking to my left, I tapped Promise on her shoulder and nodded. "Let me holla at you," I said, pushing my chair out and getting up. She hesitated, but she got up and followed me. I made a stop by the bar, grabbing an unopened bottle of Patrón and two shot glasses before leading her to the outside deck. It was closed in, so we didn't have to worry about bugs and shit. Finding the dimmer switch, I turned the lights on but made sure to keep them low. I took a seat on the padded lounge chair while she opted to sit in the chair across from me. I wasn't in a rush to talk because I really didn't know what the fuck to say. She was bouncing her leg up and down at a rapid pace, signifying that she was nervous. Popping the seal on the liquor, I poured a shot for the both of us, and shorty took that shit to the head like I just gave her some apple juice.

"Damn," I blurted. "Slow down. I don't need them thinking I'm trying to get you fucked up. Clearly you need it, though." I took my own shot and sat back with my legs gaped and one arm draped over the back of the chair.

"I don't know what you want me to say," she admitted.

"Say what you feel. How do you feel about all this shit?" I asked.

"I feel like it's stupid and I shouldn't be forced to do shit that I don't want to," she voiced. I leaned forward and poured the both of us another shot.

"Touché." I raised my glass to her and downed the strong ass liquor.

"If you feel the same way that I do, why are you doing this?"

"The same reason you probably are." Things were quiet for

a few minutes before I spoke up again. "My pops said something about a thirty-day trial. How do you feel about that?"

She shrugged. "I guess it'll give us a chance to get to know
each other."

"So, you're with that?" I asked again for clarity.

"I can deal with that," she responded.

"Aight, bet. So, check it. If we're going to do this, I need to
know who I'm going to be tied to. I'm going to get some shit in
motion and in two weeks, you're going to move in with me," I
declared.

"Wait. What? You want me to move in with you?" she damn
near squealed.

"Yeah. Why not? How else are we going to learn about each
other?" I looked at her because I thought the shit was pretty
self-explanatory.

"Knasim, I can't live with you. I don't even know you."

"But you're willing to marry me and not know me? Make
that shit make sense, shorty." I pinched my brows together
because I hope she was no dingy ass chick.

"I...I don't know, Knasim. That seems like a lot."

"I know it is. That's why I think we should move in
together, so we'll get the basics of each other out of the way.
Makes perfect sense to me, baby." My eyes bore into hers and
under the dim lights, her warm milk chocolate skin glowed. I
watched her tuck a piece of hair behind her ear as she mulled
over what I just said.

"How long do I have to think about it?" she questions.

"Two weeks. Meaning, fourteen days, and on day fifteen if
you haven't already, you'll be at my spot. My pops on some
bullshit and we have ninety days to make this shit happen. So,

what's up?" We were in a brief stare off and I watched her shoulders rise and fall before she reached for the liquor bottle and poured each of us another shot.

Raising it, she said, "I guess I'll see you in two weeks," before knocking the shot back and placing it on the table.

My pops better hope I could get along with this girl long enough to make it through the ninety days, let alone three years.

KHASIM

After talking to Promise in private, we made our own agreement to work things out. My father thought he was about to dictate every aspect of my life, but that wasn't happening. I meant what I said. If he wanted me to do this shit, I would do it my way. I haven't dated a woman since I was like twenty-three and even then; I wasn't dating her to marry her ass. Now I had to move according to how it would make my wife feel and shit. I'm not saying that it'll be hard at all. I'm just not used to the shit. Once we finished talking, we exchanged numbers and promised to stay in touch. When we got back inside, all eyes were on us.

"Did you all get to talk things out?" my father instigated.

"We decided we're going to do what's best for us, and that starts with y'all staying out of our business. We're grown and can make our own decisions regarding this relationship y'all already threw us in. Starting now, what goes on between us will be decided between the two of us. There's no need for any of you to micromanage us." I stood in front of our parents stone-faced, while Promise looked as if she was about to pass out. Maybe it was the tequila. Either way, she needed to tighten up if she was going to be my wife. I needed her to be able to speak up for herself. She wouldn't have to do it much since that's what I was for, but it would be nice to know that she could in the event that I'm not around.

"I don't think that'll be a problem as long as the guidelines are followed," my father spoke. "Promise how do you feel about what my son said?"

She looked at me, then back at our parents before saying, "I agree with Knasim."

"Very well. We'll let you two handle things your way. Thad, are you and your wife okay with that?"

"As long as my daughter agrees, then I don't see the problem."

"Then it's settled. Now let's celebrate."

"Nah. I got some shit to handle. Y'all have at it, though. Promise, come walk with me real quick." I stood and waited for her to start walking, and I followed her to the front door.

"Look, we already know this shit is a lot, but I promise to make it as bearable as possible. Maybe we can get together in a few days and go over a few things if you want. No pressure."

"I'll think about it," she replied. I nodded and left out, leaving her standing there. Knight texted me and told me to meet him at the club. His responses were short earlier, so I needed to see what that was about.

The club was packed as usual, and so was the casino. My cousins were really doing their thing with their fraction of The RCF, and I knew my uncle would be proud. When I made it to our reserved section, I saw my brother sitting by his self, nursing a bottle of Hennessy.

"Why are you sitting up here looking like somebody done pissed in your cereal?" I asked, taking a seat next to him on the other chair. He took another swig from the bottle before he answered me.

"Teyana said she's pregnant." I stopped mid motion because I knew I wasn't hearing him say what I thought he was saying. It was no way.

"Say what now? You for real?" I asked for clarity.

"That's what she told me. I was getting ready to meet y'all for dinner when she popped up at my shit, throwing fucking doctor papers in my face. I wanted to knock the shit out of her ass for that shit, but when I looked at the papers and I saw the word pregnant, I almost passed the fuck out. The fuck I'ma do with a kid? Especially one with Teyana's ass. That damn girl ain't fit to be a fucking sane human, let alone somebody's damn mama." He took another swig from the bottle and slouched further down in his seat. Shit, I didn't know what to tell his ass. I didn't have kids, but I was facing a situation I didn't particularly want to be in, so I could sympathize with that part.

"Look, I really don't know what to tell you. Did y'all talk about the shit?" I asked.

"Nah. I told her to get the fuck out of my face and I came here. I knew if I came over there, Ma and Pops would've gotten that shit out of me and I'm not ready for that shit right now. I need time to process this shit before I tell them. Ain't no need to tell them now when I know all they're going to do is the same shit that they're forcing on you, and I'll be damned. I'd run the fuck away first." I looked at his ass and started laughing, because what was that for his grown ass to say?

"Nigga, how the fuck your grown ass going to run away? Grow the fuck up. You got yourself in this shit, now suck that shit up. I told you to stop fuckin' that girl in the first place and now look. You're about to be tied to her ass for the rest of your fuckin' life because you choose to think with your dick and not use common fuckin' sense. It's no need to be pouting now. Man the fuck up, and take that shit on the chin." He huffed and rolled his eyes like a brat, but I didn't give a fuck. He knew fuckin' better.

"Whatever, nigga. How did dinner go with your fiancée?"

"That ain't my fiancée yet, but it was straight. I took her outside to talk in private, because everybody was in our fuckin' mouths and shit. We talked about the shit and agreed to try it out for the sake of the family and shit. You should be happy that I'm taking this one for the team, because it could've been you, especially now that Tey is pregnant. She's supposed to move in with me in two weeks, so that'll give me enough time to figure the shit out."

"You moving her out to The Bay or taking her to your spot in The Hills?" I thought about taking her to the condo, but if she's going to be my wife, she might as well stay at the house I had for my family.

"I hadn't thought that far ahead yet. That house is not even furnished. I'll probably bring her to the condo and let her decorate the house, since she'll be the one staying there."

"Makes sense. What about her sister?" he asked.

I frowned. "What about her?"

"You'on think that shit is weird that you fucked her sister now you're about to marry her?"

"It's not like I did the shit on purpose. Had I not seen her again so soon, I wouldn't even remember her ass. Pussy was trash anyway, so I'd say I dodged a bullet. Ain't no way in hell I'd be married to a woman with pussy as trash as hers. She would definitely get cheated on because I ain't wit' it." We shared a laugh and noticed our cousins stroll inside the section. Them niggas were always together. Maybe it was some twin shit. Me and Knight were close, but these niggas were on some 'you move I move' type shit. It was very rare that the other wasn't too far behind.

"The fuck y'all niggas up here doing?" Trig asked.

"This nigga looks like you took his favorite toy and shit. Wassup?" Murda asked.

"Nigga, done fucked around and got Teyana's crazy ass pregnant," I revealed.

"Damn," they said in unison.

"How the fuck you do that?" Murda asked.

"Nigga, you got how many kids? What you mean, how it happened?" Knight snapped.

"Fuck you. Don't get all in ya chest wit' me 'cause Unc gon' get in ya ass. How many kids I got don't matter. They're straight and nigga, my kids are by my wife. You, on the other hand, got a fuckin' bird pregnant."

"Damn, cuz. That's fucked up. What you going to do?" Trig asked.

"I ain't going to do shit and don't y'all go running y'all's mouth either. I ain't saying shit to my people yet. I need time to process this shit," he said.

"And you think Teyana's ass is going to be quiet? If so, you're dumber than I thought."

"Shut the fuck, Kyan," Knight snapped. He only called the

twins by their names when he was pissed at one of them or in the presence of our business associates.

"No, nigga. Fuck yo' crybaby ass. You better had paid for that fuckin' bottle too while you up here crying and shit." he smirked.

"So, Knas. What's up with your lil' situation. Y'all figured that shit out yet?" Trig asked. I leaned back in my seat and sighed. This shit was more annoying than I cared to admit.

"Man, we had another fuckin' dinner tonight, and I chopped it up with her and shit. We both agreed to give this shit a try for the sake of family. I got to make some adjustments, but she's supposed to move in with me in two weeks so we can start this thirty-day trial shit."

"What's supposed to happen in the thirty days?" Murda asked.

"We're supposed to get to know each other and shit. See how we can adjust to being together. It was my idea that she would move in because how am I supposed to know what I'm getting into if we don't live together? I don't need no surprises. I need to know if her ass can cook and clean and..."

"...Fuck." Knight cut me off.

"Definitely need to know that in advance," Trig co-signed, looking down at his phone.

"Watch Denver beat yo' ass," Knight voiced.

"You worrying about the wrong shit. Your main concern needs to be your ratchet ass baby mama that's headed this way." We all turned our attention to the entrance of our area. The bouncer let her through because she was Knight's girl.

"I'm out. Nigga, handle that and don't tear up my shit or expect the bill," Murda said.

"I'm out, too. Y'all niggas be easy," Trig announced, leaving behind his brother.

"What you want, Tey?" he asked. She had her cousin with her, and I took her down a few times in the past. She was easy on the eyes, but didn't have common sense first. It wasn't nothing I could do with a dizzy bitch but get my dick wet.

"I know you ain't in the club, and we have this baby on the way. You don't think you need to be making arrangements for us?" she sassed.

"Ain't you the pregnant one? The fuck you doing in here?" he snapped back.

"That's not the point. You're the man, so you need to be securing shit for our future." That shit warranted a hearty laugh from me because this bitch was delusional.

"Something funny, Knas?" she cocked her head to the side and asked.

"I ain't that nigga, Tey. Direct that shit over there." I warned. I was over her damn existence just that damn fast. Looking over at her cousin, Alicia, she had tagging along, I decided to leave, and she was going with me.

"Aye, you trying to leave?" I asked. I saw the moment her eyes lit up and chuckled.

"Uh...yeah," she answered eagerly.

"Bet. Come on." I got up to leave, and she followed suit.

"I know you're not leaving me?" Knight asked.

"I'll be next door." He nodded, and I was on my way. The club was attached to the hotel, so I didn't have to leave the building to get there. Kyan gave all of us access cards for the doors, and we had our own designated rooms. I let Alicia lead the way with my direction and we made our way through the narrow hallway connecting the two buildings. As soon as we made it into the lobby of the hotel, I ran into Precious' hoe ass. Her face housed a sneaky smirk, like she just caught me doing some shit I had no business. I went about my business to avoid her ass, but she was right on my tail.

"Damn, Knas. You going to act like you don't see me? What do you think my sister would say if she knew you were out here like this?" She twirled her finger around between me and Alicia.

"Fuck on, Precious." I grit and kept walking, but she stepped in my path.

"You know, if you let me taste that dick again, I won't say anything," she smirked.

"Bruh, you triflin' as fuck. You do see me with somebody, right?"

She shrugged. "I mean, she's cute or whatever, so I don't mind if she doesn't." I'm not even going to lie. The thought crossed my mind for a second, but disappeared just as fast.

"Man, get the fuck out of my face, and don't fuckin' approach me again," I snapped, leaving her ass right there. I led Alicia, who had been quiet the whole time, to the penthouse floor. The hotel was suite only but being a Richmond granted us our own wing and it was only penthouse suites. This particular wing was for me, Knight, and our cousins. Their other hotels were utilized by our parents.

Once we reached my room, I kicked my shoes off and placed my keys and phone on the table. I didn't drink at the club, so I headed straight to the bar that was kept fully stocked.

"What you drinking?" I asked Alicia.

"I'll take a vodka and pineapple juice," she responded. Nodding, I turned back to the bar and fixed our drinks and headed back to the sitting area. I let her sip on her drink for a few minutes before I initiated the reason why I brought her up here.

I got up and walked into the bedroom and started discarding my clothes. There was no need in me telling her to follow me. This wasn't her first go-round with me. By the time I had everything off except my boxers, she came sauntering in the room. The light coming from the lamp illuminated her honey colored skin and my dick was already straining against the material of my boxers.

"Take that shit off," I ordered. I took another sip of my drink as I watched her intensely as she rid her body of the thin material that was supposed to be a dress. She didn't have on a bra because the dress didn't require one, so her perky C cups bounced out as soon as slid the dress down over them. When she got to her hips, she had to do that lil' jiggle shit since her ass was fat and soft as fresh dough. When she discarded her thong, she exposed her neatly waxed pussy, and I appreciated the maintenance.

"Come eat this dick, and you better not play wit' it, either." I knew that was going to amp her up, that's why I said it. Like I mentioned earlier, I had no problem taking Alicia down. She was just too meek for me. Perfect example was when Precious approached us in the lobby. Granted, I don't like to cause scenes, but she could've said something. That alone only granted her access to the dick and nothing else.

I watched as she descended to her knees and fished my dick out of my boxers. She wasted no time spitting on my shit and swallowing it whole.

"Gah damn, girl. Do that shit just like that," I coached,

enjoying the feeling. She already had my toes curling and my spine tingling.

"Hold up a minute." I tapped her head so I could take my boxers off and get comfortable. Once they were discarded, she got back to work. Slurping, spitting, and moaning were the only sounds being heard as she sucked my dick like she was eager to taste my cum. After a few more times of me touching the back of her throat, I gave her exactly what she was looking for.

"Fuuuck!" I groaned, enjoying the sensation that flowed through me. When she took her mouth off of me, I went straight to the safe I had in here. Entering the code, I retrieved a box of condoms. Even though this was my personal room, people came in and out to clean and I didn't put shit past nobody. Securing my dick, I turned Alicia over, forming an arch in her back and slid right inside of her hot box.

"Mhmm," she moaned upon contact.

I took my time at first to enjoy the snug feeling her pussy provided. Shit was a B+ at best, so I could work with it. When I felt her walls tighten around me, I started drilling into her, assisting with bringing her orgasm to the forefront.

"Oh...Ga...baby...slow down," she whined.

"Shut up and take this dick." I didn't need her telling me what the fuck to do. I was running this shit. "Stop fuckin' running and throw that ass back." I slapped her right cheek hard as hell and kept hitting her spot. Moments later, she was wetting a nigga up.

"Uhm...hmm," I groaned. "Get that shit, so you can ride this dick." When I felt her walls stop convulsing, I pulled out and got on my back.

"Hurry up and get back on this dick, and you better make this shit spit, too." I tucked my bottom lip in between my teeth as she slid down on me. When she got to the base, she didn't move right away, and that was about to piss me off. I guess she read the room and started bouncing on my shit.

"This ain't no damn Po-go stick. Ride this shit like I know you know how," I ordered. That was all it took for her to ride my shit like she was a jockey in a race.

"That's it. Get this dick. Fuck...get that shit just like that." I didn't mind being vocal if the shit was worth it. I knew that shit egged women on just like it did men, and I wanted her to give me her all. The only thing she didn't have to worry about was me putting my mouth on her in any capacity. She'd have to get another nigga for that.

She started to pick up her pace, and by the way she was gripping me, I knew she was about to cum again, and I was on the verge myself.

"Gah damn, girl. Cum on this dick so I can let this shit go," I said through gritted teeth. I felt my shit coming to the surface just as she started trembling and coating a nigga's dick and pelvis with her juices.

"Oh...shit, Knas," she moaned, like she was experiencing the best orgasm of her life.

"Fuuck!" I grunted right behind her. I had to hold her in place to keep her from moving. I didn't need any more assistance after that. Once we both came down off of our high, I got up and went inside the bathroom and discarded the condom and flushed it down the toilet. When I came out, she was already dressing. She already knew I didn't do that spend the night shit, so I was glad we didn't have to go through that whole song and dance routine. I picked my boxers up and slipped them on so I could walk her to the door.

"This was nice, as usual. When can I see you again?" she asked.

"I'on know. I'm going to busy for the next few weeks." I saw the sad look in her eyes, but I didn't let that waiver me. If I fell for that with every woman, I would have a harem.

"Okay," she responded solemnly. She turned to kiss my cheek, and I backed up. The only place her mouth was allowed was my dick, yet she still tried to try her luck. I decided to stay here tonight since I had been drinking, so I took a shower and crashed. Tomorrow I will start putting things in motion for me and Promise. *Promise*. I was really about to have a whole wife out here, and I knew nothing about her ass. For her sake, she's better hope I could make it through these thirty days.

Past night went better than I expected. Knasim didn't seem that bad after all. The fact that he was fine didn't hurt either. Even though neither one of us was fond of the idea of being forced to get married to complete strangers, I'm not surprised that he made the request for me to move in with him. In a way, he was right, but I didn't know if that would be a good idea. I know men like Knasim have women coming at him in droves. There's no way that he would be able to stop that just because he's being made to.

I was done with my hygiene and was about to meet my family downstairs so we could go to brunch. I was glad that I didn't have to ride with Precious. She was already at the hotel we were meeting at. When I got downstairs, my parents were already waiting for me.

"I thought I had to come and get you," my mother said when she saw me.

"You know I don't rush my process. I'm here now and I'm ready."

"Okay, ladies. Let's go." My father came from around the corner and escorted us outside to the truck.

"Tootsie, are you excited about your new relationship?" my father asked.

"I'd hardly call it a relationship," I countered.

"I can see why you would think that, but look at it like this. You'd be doing something beneficial for the family and you gain something out of the whole ordeal," he stated.

"And what's that?" I asked. I didn't see how this was beneficial for me at all. Whatever deal he and Mr. Richmond concocted had absolutely nothing to do with me.

"You gain security," was his statement. I ignored him and continued to look for a few new things to add to my line. I had a new face cream that I was working on, but I haven't quite perfected the formula yet.

About twenty-five minutes later, we were pulling up to The Richmond Royale Hotel & Casino. I should've known this had something to do with Knasim and his family. We pulled up in front of the hotel and the valet came to receive or keys and we followed my father inside. The lobby was nice and extravagant. It had an Egyptian theme going on, and it was fitting for a family of such stature. Once we reached the restaurant, my father gave the hostess our name, and we were seated in a private area off to the side. From where we were seated, you could still see the entrance. I didn't see Precious in sight, but that wasn't unusual. She was always late.

"This is nice. Promise, just think. You could be a part of all of this," my mother voiced. She could've kept that comment because I wasn't looking for any come-ups.

"It is nice, but I'm not trying to be into all that. That's their family business," I voiced.

Before either of my parents could comment, Precious came strolling in like she was a Hollywood Scarlet.

"Good afternoon, Precious," our mother spoke.

"Precious," our father spoke.

"Oh, you're too good to speak now?" she asked me. I couldn't help the frown that formed on my face because I wasn't even bothering this damn girl and she came straight in here and chose violence.

"You didn't even give me a chance to open my mouth. What did you want me to do? Talk over Mommy and Daddy?" I snarled.

"Whatever, Promise. I forgot you're the Golden Child, even though you took my man like it's okay," she snapped.

"Excuse me?" I looked at her like she was crazy, and clearly she was. "How did I take your man? I hope you're not talking about Knasim, because I don't even want to do this shit! Had you not been on your usual hoe shit, you would have the nigga!"

"Girls! Lower your voices and calm down now!" Our father ordered. Precious sat opposite me and sucked her teeth like I really did something to her ass.

"You need to tell that to her because I didn't do anything," I challenged.

"Whatever, Promise. You think you're hot shit, but that nigga don't want you for real. I saw him here last night with another girl, and they weren't eating or gambling. He took her upstairs to a room. I saw her leave earlier, but he's probably still here waiting for the next one to show up." I couldn't say that her revealing that Knasim was with a woman last night didn't bother me, because it did. He was supposed to be marrying me, yet he was still out here doing single shit. *Was he still single?*

"That has nothing to do with me. Whatever we're doing has not started yet. So he can do as he pleases," I responded.

"Uhmm...hmm," she responded.

Just as the server came over to take our order, my phone vibrated on the table.

Knasim: You busy?

I wondered what he wanted?

Me: I'm at brunch with my family right now. I'll be free a lil' later.

Knasim: Aight. Hit me when you're done. I'll send somebody to pick you up unless you can come to me.

I wonder if he already left?

Me: We're actually at the restaurant in your family's hotel.

I saw he was typing, so he was probably wondering what we were doing here.

Knasim: Which one?

Me: The one on Richmond Way.

Knasim: Aight.

I placed my phone down because it seemed like he was done with the conversation. The server was finally around to take my order and I was ready to taste the steak bites and potatoes. When she left, my father started again, but was interrupted by an unexpected guest.

"Good afternoon," he greeted. "Promise, can I see you for a

minute?" Knasim had approached me and stood beside me with his hands in his pockets.

"Knasim, you can stay and have brunch with us if you like," my mother offered.

"No offense, Mrs. Sterling, but I'd never break bread with your other daughter if I could help it," he said without a care in the world. Precious rolled her eyes as I quickly excused myself so things wouldn't escalate. After helping me out of my seat, I grabbed my phone and followed beside him.

"Where are you taking me?" I asked as we walked out of the restaurant and into the lobby.

"To my room," he stated, and I stopped in my tracks. He turned around and noticed that I was still standing in the same spot.

He squinted his eyes and asked, "wassup?"

"I'm not going up there and you just had a girl in there?" I informed. I guess he thought I was playing because he started laughing and walking toward me. I didn't know if he was the violent type, but the way he was approaching me had me wondering.

"Let me guess. Yo' hoe ass sister told you that shit?" He cocked his head to the side. "Did she also tell you that she was also willing to join us?" He smirked and I felt foolish. I should've known that her ass was up to something. Why else would she tell me that shit?

"Did you sleep with her again?"

"I'm not talking out here. Come on." He held my stare until I started walking toward him and to the elevator. I was quiet the whole ride up. I was all of a sudden nervous. When we reached his room, I took it in, and it was immaculate. You could tell they invested a lot in making everything perfect.

I saw him press a button on the side of the wall, and a voice came through.

"Yes, Mr. Richmond. How can I help you?" I heard a lady ask.

"There's an order in the restaurant. I need you to have it sent up to my room," he responded.

"What was it, sir? I'll get right on it."

"What did you order?" he asked. I stared at him for a few seconds before I responded.

"Steak tips, potatoes, and fruit." He repeated my order and told her to double it before he hung up.

"You didn't have to do that. I was supposed to be eating with my family," I stated.

"I'm about to be family, right? Besides, we got a few things to discuss."

"Like what?"

"Like this move. I have a house that I haven't been staying in. I'll let you furnish it how you see fit. Just try not to have it all girlie and shit," he rattled off.

"Why haven't you been staying there? You stay here in the hotel?"

"Nah. I have a place out in The Bay. The house was for when I had a family, so I might as well utilize since we have to be married." He shrugged.

"If it's a family home, we don't have to stay there. It's probably too big anyway," I replied.

"You're probably right, but as your husband, it's my job to

provide and make sure that you're comfortable. I don't think the condo is big enough for that."

"You're not my husband yet, and I can make decisions for myself. The marriage will only be on paper anyway, so I don't see why we would have to stay together. You can stay at your condo, and I'll find my own place," I voiced. His brows furrowed as he looked me over. I had a pair of ripped jeans and a graphic tee paired with a pair of Air Max. The way he was looking at me had me second guessing my attire.

"How did you go from agreeing to move in with me, to wanting your own place? Where did that come from?" When I didn't answer, his face formed a smirk.

"Is this about what your sister said?" he asked.

"No. I mean...yes. Hell, I don't know. I just don't want to be in your way, is all," I stated honestly.

"Tell me the truth. Would you want me to stop fuckin' other girls?" he asked. We held our gazes for a few seconds until I broke it.

He turned my head back in his direction and said, "Look at me when I talk to you. Do you want me to stop sleeping with other women? I need to know your expectations of this shit."

I pondered on what he was asking me, and I didn't know what to say? Did I want him to be celibate? The reason I said celibate was because I was a virgin, and I didn't plan on sleeping with anybody until I got married. Thanks to Precious' ass, that's going to come sooner than I expected.

"Would you want somebody sleeping with me knowing I was about to be your wife?" I countered. His face contorted into a grimace like I offended him.

"Not unless you want that nigga dead," he stated blankly.

"So, why would you think I would be okay with you doing it?"

Silence.

The knocking on the door interrupted whatever he was about to say. I watched as he swaggered to the door and opened it. He had on a pair of gray joggers and a fitted white t-shirt with a pair of Cement Jordan fours. It was a simple outfit, but he made it look good. The person at the door rolled a cart inside the room that I assumed housed our food. I was glad to see that because I was hungry. Instead of him bringing the food back to the couch, he headed to the dining room that sat on the opposite side of where we were seated. I watched as he moved back and forth until he came back over and held his hand out.

"Come on. Let's eat." I hesitated to place my hand in his, but I did. He escorted me to the table and pulled my chair out for me to sit down before taking a seat of his own. When he sat down, he held his hands out. I looked at them before I placed my hands inside of his and he blessed the food.

"I didn't take you for the praying type," I voiced.

"How does the praying type look?" he countered.

"You're right. I'm sorry."

"It's all good. That's why we're here, so we can start to get to know one another. It's not like we have much time," he stated.

"I guess you're right. How old are you?" I asked.

"Twenty-seven. You?"

"Twenty-four." He seemed shocked to hear that.

"Damn," he grumbled.

"What is that supposed to mean?" I asked.

"Nothing. When is your birthday?"

"January 16th."

"Oh, so you just turned twenty-four," he clarified.

"Yeah. Is that a problem?"

"Nah. As long as they won't be trying to lock my ass up for fuckin' wit a minor, I'm cool."

"When is yours?" I questioned.

"December 5th."

"Back-to-back birthdays. That's interesting," I pointed out. "You have kids?" I asked between bites.

"Do I look like the type of nigga that'll have kids stashed away somewhere?"

"Actually, you do," I smirked.

"Damn, shorty," he snorted. "That's fucked up. But to answer your question, I don't have any kids. I have never fucked a girl raw in my life. I kept that reserved for my wife." The way he stared at me when he said that had my body reacting in ways it never has before.

Clearing my throat, I redirected the conversation in another direction. "What was it that you wanted to talk about?" I watched as he placed his fork down and wiped his mouth before he leaned back in his chair.

"I just wanted to feel you out without everybody around. I don't like the unknown and my pops throwing this shit on me is unwarranted, but it is what it is, so we might as well make the best of it." He shrugged.

"I get it. This wasn't exactly how I figured I'd be getting to know my husband. I thought the man I would end up marrying would be the man I fell in love with, and when he asked me, I had no choice but to say yes. I never imagined being picked out or chosen like property." I started playing around with my food because I suddenly lost my appetite.

"That's how you feel, shorty?" he asked.

"It is. Don't you feel like this is too much?"

"I do, but you know the shit our families are into, so they don't operate the same."

"I don't really know what my family does. I just know that my father always provided. I just naturally assumed he was some sort of kingpin since I never saw him go to work," I revealed, causing him to laugh.

"What?" I asked.

"That's what you think Thad does?"

"It's not?"

"That's not my place to tell you," he stated.

"Well, what is it that your family does?" I asked, sipping the orange juice that was in front of me.

"A lil' bit of everything, but we'll get into that later. I want to know what you expect from me during these thirty days." His eyes were once again boring a hole into me, like he was staring into my soul.

"All I ask is that you respect me, as if I were already your wife. Don't be out here doing things that you wouldn't want me to do," I stated.

"So, I can't fuck nobody but you?" he asked.

"You won't be fucking me either," I said matter-of-factly.

"What you mean by that?" His brows were bunched like he was genuinely confused.

"Just what I said. You won't be having sex with me either, and I won't be having sex with you until we get married." The look on his face was priceless.

"You can't be serious? You expect me to go anywhere between now and ninety days wit' no pussy?"

"That's exactly what I'm saying."

"I can't get my dick sucked either?"

"Nope. None of that." I watched as he slid down in his chair and crossed his arms across his broad chest.

"Promise, you can't be serious right now?"

"I am. Are you a sex addict or something?"

"What? Hell no, but come on, man. You can't expect me not to do anything. There has to be some kind of stipulations." I wanted to laugh because his big ass looked as if he wanted to cry.

"I mean, you can use your hands or those toys I see that they have for men." I shrugged.

"So, while I'm over here with a dry dick, what are you going to be doing?" he asked.

"Nothing."

"So you mean to tell me you're perfectly fine without sex for at least ninety days?" I knew he was going to ask that question and now I feel like just telling him he can fuck whoever he wanted, so I wouldn't look like a weirdo.

"I've waited this long...I don't see why not?" I shrugged. He stopped mid-bite and stared at me.

"Wait. You've never had sex before?" I shook my head 'no'.

"So, nobody's ever entered you?" he asked again for clarity?

"Not unless you count a tampon."

Silence.

It was awkward as fuck now, and I wish I hadn't said anything, but it was too late to take it back now.

To say I was shocked that Promise was a virgin was definitely an understatement. I mean, her sister sucked and fucked me within an hour, so I naturally assumed birds of a feather. I should've known better though because even though me and Knight were alike in a lot of ways, we were also like night and day. That nigga was really unhinged. I don't know what my parents did to that nigga, but it's obvious they did something to his ass.

"Why are you just staring at me like a weirdo? Is me being a virgin a problem for you?" she asked. I didn't even realize I was staring until she spoke up. I was too busy fantasizing about being the first man to explore her unchartered territories.

"Nah, it's not a problem. I was just surprised, that's all."

"You mean because you fucked my sister on the first night? Yeah, I'm nothing like Precious. She uses her body for everything. I was actually interested to see how y'all would have worked out," she confessed.

"Good thing we didn't. Your sister looks like the type that

would try me and then you would be an only child," I stated honestly.

"You would've hurt my sister?" she asked.

"I would've killed that bitch." I shrugged. "Enough about that, though. You in school or something?"

"Because I'm younger than you, I have to automatically be in school?" she sassed. The sudden switch in her attitude blew me because she seemed timid.

"Aye, when you got so slick at the mouth?"

"I've always spoken like this. You just haven't been around me long enough to witness it, but to answer your question, I'm not in school. I have an online beauty line. I don't sell makeup or anything. I make my own hygiene products, facial scrubs, serums, and hair products," she said, and I was impressed.

"Word? What's the name of it?" I asked.

"I-Promise."

"That's dope. So you make everything yourself?"

"Yeah. I make everything by hand. It sucks that I don't have a lot of my materials here. I wasn't planning on staying, so I guess I have to start over, or I'll have to go get my other supplies and materials." I heard her, and I was already trying to figure out how to get her shit here. I'd have somebody go pack that shit up and bring it back or we could fly out and get it. I was all for shorty making her own money.

"We'll figure all that out."

"You don't have to do that, Knasim. I'm capable of doing that myself."

"What did I tell you earlier. I like the fact that you're independent, baby girl, but you gotta let me lead while you follow. That's non-negotiable, and I promise I won't lead you astray." I know she was thrown off by my words, but I was an assertive man, and she would have to get used to it.

"So, that's how this is going to go? You're going to tell me what to do and I listen like a good lil' wife?" She cocked her head to the side.

"Not at all. You have a voice and I expect you to use it, but if I make a suggestion, I do expect you to listen and not fight me on it." He held a stern stare with me and for a slight second, I almost felt like I was melting away.

"Yes, sir. Anything else, sir?"

"I see you got jokes. Check it, though. I got to go to a few meetings today, but here...take this." I slid her the extra card to one of my accounts.

"What's this for?"

"For whatever you need. I know you need shit, and you need to furnish the house. Use that card and don't worry about the price."

"I can buy my own things, Knasim," she countered.

"Promise," I huffed. "What did we just talk about?" She didn't say anything, and I was glad.

"Did you ride with your people, or you drove?"

"I rode with my parents."

"You know how to drive?" I asked.

"Yeah," she responded.

"Aight. I'll have a car for you later. I need to go and grab some shit and I can drop you off on my way." I got up and placed the plates back on the cart.

"I can catch an Uber," she offered.

"Promise. Listen, shorty. You're about to be married to the head of a crime organization. Do you think it'll be safe or smart for you to get in an Uber, shorty? That's too accessible. Thad literally kept you green to shit that really goes on in our world. I'll change all that, though. Right now, I need to finish getting ready for this meeting." I walked off before she could have any kind of response to what I said. It only took me a few minutes to freshen up my hygiene, since I took a shower before I went downstairs. I got dressed in a pair of medium wash denim Amiri jeans, a matching olive green t-shirt and a pair of wheat colored Givenchy boots. I ran some oil through my hair and beard, and made sure my earrings were secure before clasping my watch on my left wrist and my Cuban Link bracelet on my right to match my chain. When I went back out front, Promise looked shocked.

"I thought you said you had a meeting?" she asked.

"I do."

"Doesn't look like it." She shrugged.

"Yeah, I'm not doing all that unless it's necessary. They get me the way that I am or fuck them. You ready?" I asked, picking up my keys. I made sure everything I wanted was with me and whatever I was leaving was locked up in the safe. They'd come clean the room once I left, and I'd hate to have Trig replacing his staff because they wanted to touch my shit. I escorted Promise downstairs, and we rode the elevator to the parking garage in silence. More than likely, both of us were still trying to process all of this. When we made it to the garage, I led her to my truck. I decided to drive my Limited Edition F-150 since I knew I would be handling business today.

"I didn't know this place had a parking garage," she voiced.

"How would you? This side is just for us and the staff, though. The valet cars are on the other side. If you ever come her or the club without me, this is where you'd park and use the entrance from the hotel to enter the club unless you use valet," I informed.

"Anything else I need to know?"

"Yeah. You'll have a security detail."

"Do you have one?"

"I'on need one. You, on the other hand, do. I told you once they find out about you, you may or not be a walking target. I rather have a detail on you when I'm not available to be safe."

"Is this a requirement?" she asked.

"It is. All the women affiliated with us have one. I'm pretty sure you had one too, but just didn't know it."

"I never saw anyone following me," she stated.

"They're to be felt and not seen, sweetheart. But what do you think those drivers were?" I saw her thinking about what I was saying as she looked out of the window.

The rest of the ride to her parents' house was quiet. She was probably thinking about the things I said. I made a mental note to talk to Thad about this shit. How could he have one daughter out here living recklessly and the other oblivious to what was going on around her was crazy as hell to me? He should've always had them aware of what their lives were about. Knox made sure we knew what he did for a living and so did our uncle. That way, we knew what to expect and to watch out for. Hell, Knicole even knew what our family did for a living.

I pulled up to the address she had given me, and it was in The Hills. The house I had out here was about twenty minutes from here. Pulling up to the door, I got out to help Promise out, but she had beaten me to it.

"Next time wait for me," I scolded. Her only response was a blank stare. That was cool, too. When I walked her to the door, she turned around and stopped me.

"I'm good here. Thank you for dropping me off," she offered.

"No problem, but I'm not leaving until you're inside. So go ahead and head inside for me, baby. I already told you I had a meeting." The look she gave me was one that said she wanted to challenge me, but the one I gave her in return let her know that it wouldn't be good if she did. Once she was inside, I left and headed into the office of our funeral home in The Valley. Knight was already there waiting for me, along with Trig and Murda.

"What's up, fellas?" I greeted. I went around and greeted my brother and cousins before taking a seat.

"What time is everybody supposed to be here?" I asked.

"They should be downstairs already. We were waiting for you before we headed down," Knight stated, and I nodded. Even though we all had different titles and jobs within The RCF, we all tried to attend each other's meetings because at the end of the day, we were all in this shit together.

One by one, we filed out of the office and headed downstairs to the basement where the meetings were held. When we got there, we saw that most of the guys were in attendance. I took immediate notice that Wood was missing. I looked over at Knight and I saw his jaw clenching, so I know he took notice too.

"Aye, where that nigga Wood at?" he asked nobody in particular.

Nobody responded.

"So, none of you niggas know where this nigga at" Murda asked. This nigga was the most unhinged nigga of us all.

Just before one of the guys spoke up, this nigga Wood came waltzing in like he was running shit.

"I heard you niggas were looking for me?" Wood sang as he entered the room.

"Nigga, sit yo' ol' stupid ass down somewhere 'fore I put a bullet in ya shit just for pissing me the fuck off. Nobody got time to be playing with you and your dumb ass tactics," Knight snarled.

"My bad, *Boss Man*," Wood said. I didn't trust this nigga, and that was the very reason why I watched his ass closely.

"Any fuckin' way. I called this meeting to let y'all know that we're about to be making some changes and my brother here will be the one filling you in on it," Knight announced as I walked closer to the front.

"Aight, to get straight to the point. I'm about to make some changes within the organization. Some of y'all have been working closely with me and my brother, but we're about to start some different shit."

"Now, Marco. You've been doing good running, and your hard work hasn't gone unnoticed. With that being said, we're going to promote you to the home in The Heights. That spo—"

"Aye, how the fuck you gon' give him my spot like I ain't been on my shit!" Wood roared.

"Nigga, cut me off again. I wouldn't have to replace yo' ass if you've been doing what the fuck you've supposed to be doing. Yo' shit in the middle of the hood. There's no way that the amount of dead bodies coming through that muthafucka is less than the drugs that's being pushed and the drugs are one of the highest contributors. Make that shit make sense?" I cocked my head to the side and waited for this muthafucka to dispute me. He was smart enough not to.

"That's what the fuck I thought. Like I said, Marco is taking your spot and you're going to take his." I finished.

"You give this nigga my shit, and you demote me? You niggas is crazy as he—" His sentence was cut off by a hot bullet that I shot from my Glock.

"Ahh...fuck!" he yelled out.

"I told you not to cut me off again. If you got a problem wit' that shit, then I can solve that shit permanently for you. Now, anybody else got any fuckin' complaints?" Nobody said shit, and that was the way I preferred it.

"Aight, I'm done." We all watched closely as everyone filed out of the room while we stayed behind. Wood was the last to leave, and he had a grimace on his face while he nursed his bullet wound.

"Y'all know y'all gon' need to keep a closer eye on that nigga, right?" Murda mentioned.

"Hell yeah. He gon' fuck up soon," I declared. We left from the basement and went back upstairs to the office.

"Aye, Trig. You think Denver can squeeze me in to decorate my spot?" Trig's girl was an interior designer and I know she could help Promise to decorate the house. I'm not saying I don't trust her style, but I didn't know what it was.

"You redecorating?" he asked.

"Nah. I told Promise to decorate the house so we could move in and shit," I explained.

"Damn. You really doing this shit?" Murda asked.

"That's what it looks like," I responded.

"Damn. I got you cuz. I'll make sure she's on top of shit," Trig said.

"And how do you plan to do that when you can't stay on top of y'all's shit," Knight voiced.

"What me and my girl got going on is the least of your worries, nigga. Worry about how you gon' deal with Tey's ass for the rest of your life," he shot back.

"Nah, after eighteen, I'm out."

"That's what you think. I'll have her hit you up so y'all can go over the details and shit." I nodded in agreement and got up to leave. My next stop was the dealership to cop my fiancée a new whip. Shit. I had a whole fiancée out this bitch and I didn't even know what to do with it. A virgin one at that, so I couldn't do what I wanted.

I pulled up to my boy's Tony's car lot and got out. He was the one we brought all our vehicles from so I knew he would have something that would be perfect for Promise.

"Knas. what's up, my boy?" Tony greeted me when he saw me enter the showroom.

"I know if you're in here, you're not just looking. So, what you need?" I smirked because this nigga knew me well.

"I'm glad you know. Actually, an SUV is what I need for my fiancée. Something that she can use for everyday use and for business, at least for now anyway," I revealed.

"Wait, nigga. You want something for your who?" he asked.

"You heard me. Show me what you got, and I'll fill you in."

I followed Tony around his showroom, looking at truck to truck until we stumbled across the right one. It was a pearl white 2024 Genesis GV80. I'd admit the shit was nice and it wouldn't be something that I would lean toward.

"Say, man, This shit is nice. I'm not even going to lie. It's just what I'm looking for. She has her own business and I want to make sure she has enough room to transport her shit if need be," I advised.

Nodding, he walked around the vehicle like he was expecting it before we headed into his office to go over the paperwork. When it was all said and done, I was walking out after spending close to two hundred thousand dollars after getting it fully loaded and bulletproof. She better appreciate this shit, too.

PROMISE

ONE WEEK LATER

I was getting ready to meet with Denver so we could go over a few ideas for this house Knasim was adamant that I decorate. He called and asked me did I go by and look at the place and I told him 'no'. The very next day, he picked me up and took me there for a tour. I must admit, it was a gorgeous house. It had six bedrooms, with each bedroom having its own bathroom. There were five extra bathrooms, three of them being full. The kitchen was immaculate and had a walk-in pantry that was as big as a walk-in closet. It had two living rooms, an office, an exercise room, a room designated for a game room and a nice in ground Olympic style swimming pool. The outside was just as beautiful as the inside, with a covered patio and gazebo with an outside kitchen. When I saw the master bedroom, I almost passed out. It took up an entire wing upstairs with how huge it was. There was enough room to have a living room or sitting area in there. There was even a room that resembled a small office. Off from the living room area were two rooms that were used as walk-in closets, complete with islands and vanities. The bathroom was the final stop on my tour, and I was taken aback. The interior appeared to be constructed entirely of marble. The glass shower had two separate shower heads and one waterfall one set in the middle. There was a toilet and a urinal that were set off in a small room with a sink by themselves. The huge Jacuzzi style tub sat up on a platform in front of a frosted window. The his and hers sink was a nice touch with the separate vanity. I could tell he put a lot of thought and effort into getting this built. He for sure had his family in mind and I felt guilty because he had to share it with me unwillingly. Even after telling him it was unnecessary, he refused to hear it. That's why I was getting ready to go meet with Denver to get this shit over with. I had finally gotten finished dressing when my I heard my phone ringing on the charger. When I looked, it was Knasim.

"Hello?" I answered.

"Hey. You about ready?" he asked.

"Yes. I just got finished getting dressed."

"Aight. I'll be pulling up in about ten minutes."

"Knasim, I told you I could have my dad's driver take me."

"I'll see you in a few minutes," he said, hanging up the phone in my face.

"Rude ass, nigga," I mumbled. Giving myself a once over in the mirror, I grabbed my purse and phone. When I hit the bottom of the stairs, I heard a loud, deep voice.

"Aye, back the fuck up 'fore I knock yo' shit loose, shorty. The fuck kind of shit you on?" I heard Knasim snarl, just as I made my appearance at the same time my parents did.

"What's going on here? My father asked.

"I thought I told you to keep this one on a leash?" Knasim snapped.

"Leash? Nigga, I ain't no dog!" Precious snapped.

"I can't tell. Always in a nigga's face like a bitch in heat. Watch out." He moved around her and stepped toward me. "You ready?" he asked nonchalantly, like he didn't just say my sister was a bitch.

"Uh...yeah," I responded.

"Daddy, are you really going to let him talk to me like that?" Precious quizzed.

"That nigga can't let me do shit, shorty. I treat you like you treat yourself and from day one, you presented yourself like a hoe. How else do you expect me to treat you?"

"But you fucked me, though," she retorted.

"Precious!" our mother scolded before Daddy had a chance to.

"And it was trash. What else you got because I'on have time to do this shit wit' you all day?" He stood stone-faced as she stood there fuming.

"Precious, that's enough," Daddy finally spoke up, making her stomp off.

"Knasim, I apologize for her behavior," Daddy said.

"Yeah, we'll talk about that shit later," he said.

He didn't say anything else to my father or Precious as he escorted me outside to his truck. When he got in and pulled off, I spoke up.

"Is it always going to be like this between you and my sister?" I asked. He glanced at me for a few seconds before turning his attention back to the road.

"Nah, because I plan on having no interaction with her ass after we move into the house," he stated.

"But that's my sister," I countered.

"And I fucked her," he said nonchalantly. "You okay with her being around me and trying to suck my dick every chance she can?" I hated that he made sense. I hated even more that they've been intimate.

"I thought so. I could be a grimy ass nigga and take her down, but I'm trying to turn over a new leaf since you round here making demands and shit." I didn't miss the sarcasm in his voice, but I ignored it.

"Where am I meeting Denver?" he informed me that Denver was his cousin, Kyandri's girlfriend. I couldn't lie and say that I wasn't anxious to meet her. I needed some sort of insight into what I was about to get myself into.

"At the house. I just need to make a quick stop first," he said.

I sat back silently and sent Kim a text while he drove.

Me: Girl...it was a shit show already this morning.

Bestie: What happened?

Me: Knasim came to pick me up and Precious was the one to let him in. Idk what happened before I got downstairs, but I heard him yelling at her when I did get down there.

Kim: Knowing Precious she was trying to suck that man's dick.

Me: Probably. I'll call you when I leave this damn house.

Kim: Ok boo. Ttyl.

I put my phone up and saw Knasim staring at me.

"Why are you looking at me like that?" The way he was

looking had me second guessing my outfit. I had on a tank style olive green romper and gold Chanel sandals. It was simple enough to do whatever I had to do today.

"Because I can. I know you better not be texting another nigga in my shit," he stated.

"Excuse me? We're not married yet, so who I talk to is none of my business."

"Don't play wit' yours or that nigga's life, shorty." He didn't say anything else as I noticed we pulled up to a car dealership. He parked his truck and rounded the front and held his hand out to help me out.

"I could've stayed in the truck while you handled your business," I offered, and he ignored me. He stopped in front of the entrance and opened it for me to go inside. When we were inside, I saw a handsome man smile and approach us.

"Knas, my boy. You're right on time. We just got finished cleaning everything up for you. It'll be pulled out front in a few minutes," he stated.

"'Preciate it. Uh...this is Promise," he awkwardly introduced me.

"Damn," the guy mumbled, or at least he thought he did.

"Aye, watch that shit," Knasim snapped.

"My bad, but you lucked up, nigga. Nice to meet you, Promise. Your fiancé is an asshole. I'm Troy."

"Nice to meet you, Troy," I greeted.

"Here y'all go," he said and headed toward the door. Knasim followed suit, escorting me along the way. When we got outside, we were standing in front of a nice SUV. It looked expensive as hell.

"Looks good, don't it?" Troy asked with a smirk.

"It does. Why did you bring me here if you were buying a new truck? You seem to have plenty already. I could've stayed in the truck or waited until you were done," I mentioned. Since I've met him, I've already seen him in three trucks, including the burnt orange Range Rover.

"I ain't do none of that because it's yours." He opened the door for me and stood beside it like he was waiting for me to get in.

"What?" I asked incredulously. "You bought me a truck? Why?" I rambled off.

"Because you needed your own shit. I figured the truck would be good for business and shit," he said, never taking his eyes off of me.

"Knasim, I can't take this. This truck looks expensive and I—,"

"Promise." He said my name like he was annoyed. "I think you forgot what I said, shorty. This is non-negotiable. Damn, can you at least say thank you instead of always complaining?" He had his handsome face balled up, and I wanted to protest a little more, but he had a way of shutting that down without even opening his mouth. Slowly, I walked over to the truck, and he assisted me into the driver's seat. It seemed as if I melted as soon as my butt hit the leather seats. While I ran my hands over the steering wheel and admired the interior, I was slowly falling in love.

"It's nice, huh?" Troy interjected.

"It's okay," I smirked.

"Damn. I can't get no props, huh?" Knasim pouted.

"Okay...okay. I like it. I still think it's too much, but it's nice. Thank you."

"'Bout time you show some manners, and you're welcome, shorty. I got some shit to do, but go ahead and meet with Denver and call me if you need me."

"Okay." He shut the door and watched as I put on my seatbelt and adjusted my mirrors. That's when I noticed an all-black SUV parked on the other side of his truck. After putting the address to the house into the GPS, I pulled out of the parking lot and, sure enough, so did the SUV.

And so it begins.

————

When I got to the house, I pulled up, and the gate opened like Knasim informed me it would. I remember him telling me that all his cars were equipped with sensors that allowed him to enter his homes, as well as his brother, cousins, and parents' homes. I'm assuming this one had one for this house. When I drove up the long driveway, I parked right behind a black Maybach S 580 parked in the circular part. The person inside, who I assumed was Denver, got out and approached me.

"Hey, girl. You must be Promise? I'm Denver," she greeted, sticking her hand out for me to shake it.

"Nice to meet you, Denver," I greeted.

"Likewise. Now, let's go in here and see what we can do before I have to shoot your big ass fiancé, then his cousin, because I know he's going to start his shit if I do." I laughed a little as I followed her to the front door. Knasim had already programmed my handprint for the knob when I came over with him, so I didn't have a problem gaining access. Once inside, she went straight to work.

"So, Promise. Where do you want to start?" she asked.

"Uhm. I would think the living room. It's the first thing you see once you walk through the foyer and small hallway," I said.

"Perfect. Now, Knasim has these big ass windows up front like he's white, but you can't see in from the outside. Are you a bright and sunny person or a dark and gloomy one?" she asked.

"Whatever you think he'll like would be fine with me." I shrugged. She stopped doing whatever she was doing on her phone and looked up at me.

"Listen, Promise. I know all about the situation with you and Knas. Hell, if I'm being honest, I wish they had made Kyandri do what they're making Knas do. Then maybe I wouldn't want to kill him every other week. I know it's not ideal, but baby, if you're here, then you agreed. This is your life now. You're a part of The RCF, and your future husband will be the head of the organization. I'm going to need you to start acting like the First Lady and make the best of this situation. Look at it like this. You'll be married to a fine man, despite his nasty ass attitude and rude mouth. He's not that bad at all. His money is longer than the square root of pi and he's giving you free rein to do as you please to this house. Take advantage, sis'." I heard what she was saying, and I hated to agree with her. I agreed to do this for my family, so I needed to make the best of the situation while I was in it.

"Thank you. Nobody ever sat down and took the time to rationalize things for me. My parents keep pushing me to go along with it and Knasim just makes demands. It's nice to have someone sort of in my position in my corner."

"You're welcome. You have my number and after today, I hope you plan on using it. Now, let's go spend this nigga's money," she laughed. I followed her from room to room, giving her my best ideas to bring the vision I was going for to life. By the time we went through every inch of the house, I had picked out items for every room and bathroom. I had all the kitchen appliances that weren't already installed ordered, even down to the robot vacuum cleaners.

When we left, I promised to keep in touch and headed back to my truck. As soon as I was inside, Knasim's name popped up on the dash's screen.

"Hello?" I answered.

"Damn. For someone who didn't want to move in the house, you damn sure ain't just spent money like you didn't," he said through the speakers. By the tone of his voice, I could tell he was joking.

"Well, I figured it was time that I got used to this lifestyle. You know?"

"Yeah, I know it sounds like you've been talking to Denver's ass because that sounds just like her. It's all good though. As long as you're comfortable with everything that you chose, then I'm cool," he stated.

"Thank you."

"No need to thank me. When did they say they would start delivering things?"

"Denver put a rush on everything, and some things are set to arrive as early as tomorrow. Friday should be the last day for everything." I informed him of everything that Denver had told me.

"Aight. I know Denver will be emailing or texting you about

deliveries. Just let me know ahead of time if you can so I can be accessible. I want to make sure them niggas don't fuck up my shit."

"Got it. Anything else?" I asked.

"Nah. Not that I can think of. Let me get ready for this meeting, though. I'll hit you up a lil' later."

"Okay." When he hung over the phone, I mulled over the fact that this was really happening. I was about to be married to this man in less than ninety days and that alone made my stomach churned. I just furnished a whole house for us to live in together and that was huge for me. I guess I need to finally get out of my head and prepare to become the First Lady of The RCF.

––––––––

I didn't go straight home. I found another natural boutique that sold some of the items that I used for my products and went to go check them out. I ended up with a few things so I could test them out and see if I would have any use for them. When I pulled back up to the house that my parents were staying in, Precious was walking out the door, but stopped when she saw me get out of the truck that Knasim had gifted me.

"Oh, you driving his shit now?" she questioned with her voice laced with as much attitude as she could muster.

"No, I'm not. As a matter of fact, that's the truck that he brought for me," I stated, pushing past her to get inside.

"He brought you a truck!" she yelled. "You must've gone

over there and sucked that nigga's soul out if he's doing all of that?"

"Actually, I'm not doing anything. I don't need to degrade myself to get men to do things for me. I know you hate that, but that's not my fault. I didn't say anything all those years when they preferred you over me, so what's your problem, Precious?" I was sick of her acting like I did some shit to her.

She came back into the house and slammed the door. "My problem is you acting like you didn't want to come on this trip, but jumped at the chance to get with my man! You knew this arrangement was supposed to be between us and had he not ran into you; we could've worked something out!" I looked at this girl like she had lost her mind. By now, our mother had come to see what all the noise was about.

"Girls! Why are y'all out here yelling like you're crazy?" she asked as she approached us.

"Precious is blaming me for things not working out for her and Knasim," I said.

"She's flaunting what he did for her in my face," she lied.

"How did I do that, Precious? All I did was get out of my truck and you jumped to conclusions thinking it was his and I simply told you that it was mine that he gifted me. You started with me."

"Precious. We've been over this over and over again. You got yourself out of the arrangement because of your antics. I can't say I blame Knasim because we didn't raise you that way. You didn't even know the man or his name, yet you slept with him. How did you think he would be okay with that? You need to get over it and stop blaming Promise. You caused all of that on yourself, so deal with it," our mother stated with finality.

"Whatever. You're always taking up for her, anyway. I'll do everybody a favor and just stay out of the way." With that, Precious stormed out the door, proceeding to slam it, leaving me and my mother standing there.

"Well, let her go cool off and come show me this truck your fiancé brought you." She smiled. It was rare that we shared moments alone but when we did. I soaked them up because I never knew when another chance would present itself.

KNASIM Ten

I'd been busy most of the week trying to set things straight with the new arrangements I made within the organization. We had to get Marco set up at the home in The Valley while we switched up a few routes to get Wood's ass accustomed to shit. I had a few eyes on his team that would keep a closer eye on him for me. Knight couldn't stand nor trust that nigga and wanted to go ahead and end his ass right there on the spot. Under any other circumstances, I wouldn't have a gave a fuck, but with me transitioning to the front seat, I had to think more rationally.

While I was setting things straight with the homes, I had to get Thad up and running. I wasn't doing that until I had a conversation with him, though. I hadn't seen Promise much, but she did tell me about the altercation between her and Precious. I needed this nigga to get his other daughter under control before I did that shit for him. Hence the reason I was on the way to the house in The Estates. That's the house my father normally operated out of, and that's where this little meeting would be held. When I got there, his receptionist, Jessica, was sitting at her desk and greeted me when I walked in. There was no need for her to announce me because I knew where I was going, and they were expecting me. When I walked in, the two of them were talking and all of that ceased the moment I crossed the threshold.

"Hello, son," my father spoke.

"What's up, Pops. Thad." I nodded, and he returned the gesture.

"We are about ready to set up routes for Thad, but you said you needed to talk to him first," My father stated.

"Yeah. I need to set a few ground rules before I agree to anything else. I already got bamboozled once." I glanced at my father. "Thad, before I continue with this merger, I need you to get Precious' ass under control. I know we met under less appropriate circumstances, but I'm going to need you to get her ass in check before it be her organs that you're trafficking," I stated matter-of-factly.

"Wait a minute, Knasim. Are you threatening my daughter?" he asked with way too much bass in his voice for my liking.

"Clear ya throat and watch how you talk to me. I'm not threatening shit. I'm telling you if you don't get that bitch in line...I will. Promise has one more time to tell me she approached her on some bullshit and we're going to have a real serious problem that nobody walking this side of the Earth can get you out of." I held my glare with him to let him know just how serious I was.

"Those are my daughters, and they will have disagreements. It's been like that their whole lives," he explained.

"And Promise is now my fiancée, and it's my job to make

sure she's good. I mean, this arrangement was all your idea, right?" I smirked. I looked over at my father and he had a look of pride plastered on his face.

Sighing in defeat, he finally responded. "I'll talk to Precious, but I can't make any promises. The girl is bullheaded."

"You better figure the shit out. Another thing. You need to tell Promise what you do before I do. She thinks you're some kingpin. I have no plans on lying to my wife, so if you don't tell her and she asks me...I'm telling her. Play ya hand, Thad. I don't like repeating myself and for the best interest of everybody involved...don't make me." I stared at him blankly as he stared back before he nodded his head in agreement.

"Will there be anything else, son?" my father asked.

"Nah. I'm about to go and make sure the rest of my things are delivered to the house and meet Promise over there. Everything is done, and this will be our first night staying there," I stated.

"Good...good. I'm glad that you're finally getting on board with everything," he responded.

"It's not like you gave me much of a choice," I countered.

Since I said everything that I needed to say, I left my father and Thad to sit back and figure their shit out. If he knew better, he'd school his boy on the new son-in-law he'd acquired because I'd hate to have to console Promise at his funeral, but I would. Before I went to the house with Promise, I stopped by my parents' house to holla at my mother. She had been standing in the paint for me to make sure things got situated with the house since I was busy. Between her, Denver, and even Knicole's worrisome ass, things moved smoothly and a lot less stressful for Promise.

I pulled through my parents' massive gate and parked my truck behind Knicole's car. When I got inside, I followed the voices. I found my mother, Knicole, and my Aunt Syrena sitting around laughing and drinking wine.

"Sounds like y'all up to something," I said, making my presence known.

"You might be right," my mother said after I kissed her forehead before doing the same to my aunt and sister.

"We're planning your engagement party," she said.

"My what? Come on, Ma. I don't want all that," I groaned.

"Stop whining like a baby. Promise might want it," Knicole inputted.

"Have you asked her before you even started planning?" I asked, and all three of them were looking dumb in the face.

"I thought so. And Aunt Rena, if you're here, that means you plan to host it in the ballroom of the hotel." Her sly grin gave her away.

"Man," I dragged out. "Can y'all at least wait until I talk to her and see what she says. Y'all taking us too fast, and we're already moving fast enough."

"Well, I guess I can do that. I need to get with Lydia, anyway. I don't want to leave her out," my mother reasoned.

"Thank you. Now, is everything at the house or do I need to go to the condo and get anything?" I asked.

"I took the rest of your clothes and shoes by the house earlier. I told Promise to let you put your own shit up, but her OCD ass did it, so I helped her." Knicole shrugged.

"You better not had taken none of my shit. You know how your fingers like to stick to shit that doesn't belong to you. I bet not see one of my shirts turned into no damn dresses either, Knic." I scowled at her ass, and all she did was shrug.

"Everything looks nice, son. Let me know if you need my help with anything else. Have Promise call me as soon as you talk to her so we can get a roll on things."

"Aight. I'm out." I kissed the ladies and headed out. For some reason, I was nervous as hell about going home. For one, I knew it was the start of some permanent shit. Instead of heading straight there, I made a detour to Knight's house. I knew he was home because he mentioned having his security sensors changed and he needed to be home for that.

I got to his house and buzzed him at the gate since my sensor no longer worked. I knew he looked at me on the camera and let me right in. I walked inside in this nigga was in here cooking and listening to old school R&B songs. That was our shit, though. Every time our mother cooked, she turned her music on and got to work. I guess she passed that down to us.

"What you in here burning up?" I quizzed, taking a seat at his counter.

"You sound like a hater because you know I ain't burning shit. But since you asked, I'm frying me some wings." I nodded because whether he knew it or not, I was getting in on that.

"Well, I hope you got enough. You heard from Teyana?" I asked.

"Nah. I haven't seen her since the night at the club," he responded.

"You don't think you need to check in on her if she's pregnant with your kid?"

"Clearly she doesn't think she needs to check in with me and she's *allegedly* pregnant with my kid. I'm not about to let

Tey's crazy ass stress me. She'll hit me up when she's ready." I didn't argue with him, because if anybody knew my brother, I did. He didn't like to be cornered into shit, and I wasn't going to be the one to do it.

"I feel you. But listen. I need to talk to you about something." He placed a few pieces of the wings on a plate covered with a paper towel before dropping a few more pieces into the hot grease.

"Wassup up?" he asked.

"Man, Promise is a virgin," I blurted out. He stared at me for a few seconds before a stupid grin plastered on his face.

"You lucky ass nigga. You get to train and teach her ass to become the perfect freak for you," he voiced.

"Too bad that won't be happening no time soon," I revealed.

"What you mean by that?"

"She doesn't want to have sex until we're married."

"Yo, you for real?" he quizzed.

"Yep. She even said I couldn't fuck other bitches. The fuck I'm gon' do with a dry dick for three months?" I was already stressed the fuck out. It had already been about two weeks since I slid into something warm and tight, and it wasn't enough lotion and cold showers in the world.

"Damn. So, what you gon' do?" he asked.

"I thought about tricking her ass, but I can't do that, so I guess I got to stick it out until after we're married." I shrugged.

"And when was the last time you had some?"

"About two weeks ago," I admitted.

"Damn! I hate that for you, my boy, but you can stick that shit out. You know Pops raised us to respect our women and shit so y'all need to figure out what works for y'all. She may be willing to compromise if you can come up with some shit that doesn't require you to penetrate her. Use your imagination, nigga." I heard what he was saying, and I actually thought about it, but I didn't think she would go for it. Especially after calling me a sex addict. That shit rubbed me the wrong way because that shit sounded sick as fuck.

"Yeah, I'll figure it out. Come up off some of those wings, though, before I go. Tonight is our first nice in the house and I want to be there at a decent time and shit," I mentioned.

"Look at you. Already being a sucker ass nigga," he chuckled, and I had no choice to join in with him because he was right in a sense. I was just trying to do right and respect her as she requested.

———

It was weird as hell coming home to somebody, especially when that person was my fiancé. The smell of the ocean hit my nose as soon as I walked inside. When I walked through the small hall, I noticed that it was a candle burning on a table that sat along the wall. The further I went in; I saw that there was another candle lit on the glass circle table that sat in the middle of the living room. I hadn't been over here much, but Promise and Denver really hooked this shit up nicely. The living room was gray and navy blue with hints of gold. That was the scheme throughout the whole lower level. Just different patterns and shades. Before going upstairs, I checked the entire downstairs to make sure everything was in place and secured. It wasn't that late, only around seven, but you could never be too careful. Once I secured the area, I headed upstairs; I checked all the rooms, and they were all spotless and made up like someone would be occupying them. When I got to my bedroom, it was spotless, yet empty. I saw Promise's car in the garage when I pulled in, so I knew she was here. Pulling out my phone, I called her to see where she was.

"Hello?"

"Aye, where you at?" I asked as soon as I heard her voice.

"I'm at the house."

"I'm inside the house, shorty, and I didn't see you."

"That's because I'm in the basement," she huffed. I didn't even respond. I hung up and headed back downstairs and headed to the basement. When I got there, I was shocked to see her down there like she was in a mini lab.

"Wait...wait. What you doing down here?"

"Making some shampoos," she responded.

"You couldn't do that upstairs, shorty? This was supposed to be my man cave, and you done turned it into a sweatshop," I frowned.

"Well, I asked you did you have any requirements or restrictions and you said 'no'. I took that as I could do as I pleased as long as I was comfortable. This made me comfortable." She shrugged.

I looked around, and she really had everything lined up on shelves and tables. We sent for her equipment, and she even got a few new things, and they were set up as well. The basement was equipped with a full kitchen and bathroom and an extra laundry room and entrance. Almost like a separate apartment.

"Man, you should've asked me before you did this shit.

Now, where am I supposed to go when I got company?" I asked, with a frown etched on my face.

"Did you look at everything when you came in?" she asked.

"Nah, I didn't."

"It's obvious," she sassed. I watched as she wiped her hands off and sashayed past me and out the door and up the stairs. I assumed that was for me to follow her. She was in some small shorts and crop top that I wanted to rip off her ass, but I refrained. When I got to the top of the stairs, she was headed down the hallway where the game room was located. When I got there, she had already had the lights on and standing off to the side. The sight before me made me feel like a complete asshole for coming at her the way that I did. She had transformed the room I designated for a game room into a man cave. It was equipped with a bar setup, pool table, darts station, a card table and four flat screens mounted on the walls. There were black recliners and two small sofas in the room. When I looked at her, she had a blank expression on her face.

"My bad, shorty. I shouldn't have come at you like that. You're right. I told you to do whatever you wanted, and you did. This shit is dope, and I appreciate it."

"You're welcome. Even though I should return all this shit. I'm not though because it wasn't my money that paid for it," she smirked.

"Ha! You're right. But for real. I like this." I pulled her into my body and wrapped my arms around her and gave her a hug. The moment I felt her body pressed against mine; I felt a pull that had me stepping back.

"Uh...you ate anything yet?" I asked.

"No. I was busy getting everything together so I could make my day fifteen deadline," she smirked.

"You're prompt, I like that. Look, go upstairs and get ready and I'm going to take you to dinner and shit. I feel like I owe you that much since you put all this shit together without me, even though it was my money that got the job done." We both shared a laugh.

"I can do that. How do I need to dress?" she asked.

"You still got that orange dress?" I smirked, and she blushed.

"I do."

"Good. Wear that."

"Okay."

I watched as she sauntered out of the room, leaving me with my thoughts. If she knew what the fuck I was thinking, she wouldn't look at me the same. I don't know how I was going to do it, but I had to get through the rest of this bullshit ass trial run and not being able to touch her like I wanted was going to make it hard as hell.

KNASIM
Eleven

I followed Promise upstairs and I couldn't take my eyes off of her voluptuous round bottom. It's a shame and a blessing that no one had the chance to experience that shit yet. I can just imagine how much it'll ripple up against me as I stroked her from the back. When we got inside of the room, I told her to go ahead and shower while I got her clothes ready. To cut time down, I showered in another bathroom. Another reason was because Promise had my dick hard as hell and I needed to relieve that pressure before going back around her. Once I drained my nuts and washed my ass, I went back into the bedroom to find Promise sitting on the chaise in front of the bed, putting oil on her skin. She was only in her bra and panties and that sight alone was enough to say fuck dinner. But then I had to quickly bring it back in, so I just went to the dresser to find an undershirt, socks, and a pair of boxers.

"Your boxers and socks are in the top right drawer and your undershirts are in the one next to it," she revealed. I glanced back at her before going into the drawers that she mentioned.

Pulling out a pair of boxers, I went into the closet to slip

them on and change. Since she was wearing the orange dress I
suggested, I decided to compliment her with a pair of brown
washed jeans and a beige t-shirt with orange and brown
designs. Looking over to the wall that displayed my shoes, I
chose a pair of tan Prada sneakers. I picked up my brown Patek
watch and slipped it on my wrist and clasped my Cuban Link
necklace and bracelet on. When I walked out of my closet, I
didn't see Promise.

"Promise," I called out.

"In here!" she responded.

I followed her voice to the closet that was reserved for her,
and I saw her standing in front of the mirrored wall, trying to
zip up her dress.

"Why didn't you ask me for help instead of coming in here
acting like you got gummy bear arms?"

"You were getting dressed, and I didn't want to bother
you."

"Listen, whenever you need me...no matter what it is...let
me know and I'll always do what I can to make it happen.
Aight?"

"Okay," she simpered.

"Cool, now turn around."

As she turned around, I let my eyes do what they do and
take all of her in. I couldn't help the way that my hands gravi-
tated to her hips and grazed her body as I found the zipper and
pulled it up. I let my hands linger a little while longer, and both
of us were just staring at each other in the mirror until she
stepped away.

"Uh...thank you. I need to finish getting ready," she
announced. Nodding, I went into the room to grab my phone,

wallet, and keys before I headed downstairs to wait for her to finish. While I was sipping on the drink I fixed, Knight was calling.

"Wassup?" I answered.

"So, how's the house?" he asked as soon as our call connected.

"Man," I drawled out.

"It's that bad?" he quizzed.

"Shit...hell nah. Promise did her big one. This shit is nice as fuck. I'm definitely shooting Denver something for getting this shit done in the short amount of time that she did and has it looking like this." It was true. There's no way a normal person could get this big ass house furnished in a week and it looked like this. I don't think there was anything left to do, but I could be wrong.

"Damn, nigga. I need to come check that shit out soon, then. You know, pick out my room and shit," he joked.

"Fuck out of here. You ain't getting no room over this bitch when you got a house damn near the same size."

"Whatever. You in for the night?" he asked.

"Nah. I'm actually taking Promise to dinner as a thank you for getting this shit done," I mentioned.

"Ol' sucker ass nigga. Ain't even married yet and acting like a simp." We shared a laugh.

"Fuck you. I ain't acting like...shit," I couldn't even finish my sentence because Promise came into view and looked like a fuckin' chocolate goddess. That dress didn't do her any justice. If anything, it should be honored to be that close to her body. Her skin looked like it was shimmering, and I couldn't tell if she had on makeup or not, but I did notice the shine to her lips. She had her long, dark hair up in a bun, showcasing her pretty ass face.

"Yeah, I'll hit you back later," I said into the phone and hung up in Knight's face.

"I'm ready," she announced.

"I see. Promise, I'm telling you now. You look sexy as fuck and it's taking every ounce of restraint that I possess not to rip that shit off of you and do everything unimaginable to you right now. You ain't making this easy for me, baby girl," I spoke, licking my lips in the process.

"I'm not trying to entice you, Knasim. It's rare that I go out, so I wanted to look good. I'll take what you said as a compliment and say thank you."

"You got it, shorty. Come on, let's get out of here before I change my mind and you let go of all your morals." I escorted her out of the bar area with my hand on the small of my back and led her outside to the garage. I bypassed her truck and my two other two vehicles. I was glad I had a ten car garage built because I needed my babies close by. I'm glad I could depend on my mother and Knic to bring my shit. Which reminds me, I needed to check my shit.

I walked over to my white mango Mercedes-AMG GT 63 S and opened the door for Promise to get inside. After I made sure she was in and I comfortable, I went around and got into the driver's side.

"How many cars do you have?" she asked as I opened the garage and backed out.

"Five. Three trucks, and two cars. The F-150 and the Escalade are my everyday rides. I only pull the cars out on special occasions," I revealed.

"This is nice. The car I had back home was a Mercedes, but it wasn't as nice as this one. I don't know if I love this one or Denver's the most."

"You have access to my shit, so if you want to drive this one...you can."

"You don't have to do that. You already brought me the truck. You don't have to let me drive your car," she stated.

"What did we talk about?" I asked, glancing over at her.

Silence.

"Promise," I said, a little more sternly.

"That you got me," she sassed.

"Aight. So if I say it's cool to drive this car or any of other ones...you can. Stop fighting me at every angle, shorty, or this shit will be more tumultuous than it needs to be." I looked at her when I stopped at a red light and just admired her beauty. The honking cars behind me broke me out of my trance and I headed to the restaurant.

"This is nice," she cooed as we pulled into the restaurant's parking lot.

"Thanks," I smirked.

"This is yours?" she asked, shocked.

"Yeah. Me and Knight own it together," I responded.

I got out of the car and went over to her side to help her out. When we got to the front, the hostess directed me to my private area outside on the patio, facing the water.

"This is beautiful."

"This ain't got shit on my view," I flirted.

"Could you stop? You don't have to do all that with me. We already know what this is," she countered.

"And that constitutes me to being blind. One thing you'll

learn about me is that I'll never do or say anything that I don't mean. Chill and let me flirt a lil' bit since that's all I can do," I smirked.

She got quiet when I said that, and I could see the wheels turning in her head. The waiter came out to ask Promise's drink order. There was no need to ask for mine since they had it memorized. When he left, I put my attention back on Promise.

"Wassup? Looks like you want to get something off of your chest." She looked off out at the water and sighed.

"Promise," I demanded.

"Are you still sleeping with other women? I mean, I don't blame you if you were, but I'm not going to lie and say that it wouldn't bother me. I know what we have isn't a real relationship per se, but if we plan on being married, I would hope that you still respected it," she said. I took her in for a few minutes before I started talking.

"I thought we cleared that up the other night?" The waiter brought her drink back, and she took a sip before looking back at me.

"We did, but—,"

"Ain't no buts, shorty. You gave me your expectations, and I agreed with them. I wasn't raised to treat the woman that I'm in a relationship with like my side bitch. Cheating ain't in me, baby. This shit may not be ideal, but it is very much so a relationship. One that will lead to us being husband and wife. I honor that shit like I honor God. So, to answer your question, no I haven't been with anyone since we had our talk. Is it frustrating? As fuck, and that's only because I can't get a hold of you like I want. I showered in another bathroom earlier to one, save time, and because I needed to relieve the pent up tension that you caused walking around in those lil' ass shorts." I smirked. "Now, can we enjoy tonight?"

"We can do that. Will you tell me what it is that you do? This restaurant is definitely not affording multiple hundred thousand dollar cars and a mini mansion." Placing my drink down on the napkin, I leaned back in my chair and stared at her for a minute, trying to gather my words in my head before I spoke.

"My grandfather was a mortician. He started his first funeral home when he was twenty -five. He inherited it from his father. Not only was he a mortician, he was a hustler, but very few people knew. He had a few connections and started to build up his own team. Over time, those teams grew, and some branched out on their own. The collective families formed alliances with my family being the head. The RCF is one of the largest crime organizations in the Western Hemisphere. Everything comes through us. Drugs, weapons, money...you name it. We got it." I watched her intensely to see how she would react to what I just told her.

"I figured it was something like that. Y'all not into trafficking, are you?" she asked.

"Hell nah. That's some sick shit, but we are looking into a branching into a similar business. It still has a few kinks to work out, though." She nodded.

"Your mom and sister seem nice. Knicole said we would get together and hang out once I got settled in," she revealed.

"Good luck wit' that. Knic is about to run you raggedy if you let her," I laughed.

"Speaking of my mama. How do you feel about an engagement party? This lady was actually starting to plan everything, but I had to put a stop to it. I didn't want her doing things that you wouldn't be comfortable with."

"I mean, that is a part of the process, right? I'm pretty sure my mama would like that. Any excuse to spend money is right up her alley."

"Cool. I'll let her know that she can finish whatever she was planning and to hit your mama up." She nodded her head in agreement. The waiter came back out and took our order and we continued to talk while we waited for our food.

"So, what's your favorite color?" she asked.

"You sound corny as fuck right now, but it's black."

"Why black?" she asked.

"Because it's mysterious, and it goes with every damn thing."

"Makes sense. What about your favorite food?"

"Chicken."

"Typical," she laughed.

"How so?"

"Niggas love chicken," she laughed again.

"Whatever. What's your favorite color?"

"Brown."

"I can see that. What about food?"

"Not really a food, but I love Tootsie Rolls. Don't ask me why...I just do. It's the reason my daddy calls me Tootsie," she revealed.

"Fuck out of here," I laughed. "Your pops call you Tootsie?"

"He does," she said with attitude. "Your parents don't call you by a nickname?"

"Hell nah. They call me what the fuck they named me. But Tootsie is cute though. It fits," I said, and she blushed.

The waiter came back and brought our dishes out. I ordered a Tomahawk steak with double loaded mashed potatoes, while Promise had a ribeye with grilled shrimp skewers and lobster macaroni and cheese. I held my hands out and waited for her to place hers into mine and I blessed the food.

"This is good," she complimented.

"It took us forever to vet the best chefs and I think we got the pick of the litter because they all are beasts in the kitchen."

We continued to eat and enjoy the company that the other provided. I was dead against this shit, but Promise being the person that she is makes this shit easier.

"Did you enjoy yourself tonight?" I asked as we pulled back into the garage of our home.

"I did. I appreciate you taking me out."

"No problem, shorty." Cutting the car off, I got out to retrieve her and escorted her inside. Once we were upstairs, she went into her closet, and I went into mine. After finding a pair of basketball shorts, I went to search for Promise. I found her in the bathroom, rubbing something into her face. I went into the stall and peed. When I flushed, I went to wash my hands before leaning up against the sink.

"What you got going on in here?"

"I'm doing my nightly routine," she revealed.

"Is that shit going to come off on my sheets and shit?" I asked with a frown. I was all for her sticking to her routine, but I didn't want that shit in my bed.

"No, smart ass. I don't sleep in any products that rub off or stain."

"Good. What's this you doing now?" I asked.

"Just cleaning the little bit of makeup I had on off. Once I rinse that off, I'll use a serum to lock in the moisture and apply a face mask that I'll wash off in the morning."

"A mask?"

"Not an actual mask, but when I apply it, it dries clear and I sleep in it," she responded. I guess that was cool. Shit, her skin looked good as fuck.

"You think you can hook your boy up. I can't have you out here outshining me and shit." I smirked.

"I have some of my men's collection in the basement. When I'm done, I'll go get it for you." I nodded and stood and watched her like a creep as she did every step that she explained to me. It didn't hurt that she was in another pair of those little ass shorts and an even smaller tank top that exposed her pierced belly button and nipples.

She was finally done with her face and had headed downstairs to the basement to grab the products for my face. She came back with a basket of shit that had me wondering was she about to put all that on my face.

"You about to use all that?" I asked.

"No. I brought a few since I didn't know what type of skin you had. Sit on that stool for me, so I can reach your face." I looked down at the small ass stool that I looked like it would break if I propped my foot up on it.

"Shorty, my big ass won't be able to sit on that lil' ass shit without busting my ass."

"Well, I can't reach your face like that unless you follow my instructions and do it yourself," she sassed. Glancing down at her, I wanted to pinch her pierced nipples so badly, but I refrained. Instead, I scooped her up by her underarms and sat her on top of the counter.

"Ahh," she yelped.

"Now, that's better." I wedged myself between her legs and watched her breathing hitch. She quickly got herself together and cleared her throat. It was my turn to get all hot and bothered when she placed my face in between her petite hands and inspected it while she rubbed her thumbs delicately over my cheeks.

"You look like you have combination skin, but it's not bad."

"What does that mean?" I questioned.

"It means that it's oily in some spots and dry in others. I'm going to exfoliate you first to remove all the dead skin. Then maybe a light cleanser and with the serum and mask."

"That sounds like a lot of shit, Promise." I frowned.

"It's not, and once you get used to it, you'll breeze through it." I didn't know what she was talking about, but I shit up and let her pull out a small cotton ball looking thing that expanded into a washcloth when she wet it.

"Oh shit. Look at you with the face gadgets and shit," I chuckled. You would think I never washed my damn face before, the way I was relishing in the way that she was wiping my shit.

The exfoliating shit wasn't that bad, and the cleanser tingled. Everything had a woodsy scent to it, and I appreciated it not smelling like a damn woman.

"What do you put on your beard?" she asked. I looked at the counter to see if I had seen the little bottle, but it wasn't there.

"It's an oil that I was buying from this boutique in town. Why?"

"I just asked. I'm not sure what you were using, but I know mine is better."

"Oh really? You think so?"

"I know so," she gloated. She poured a small amount of oil in her hands and rubbed them together before she started to apply it to my beard and massaging it at the same time.

"This shit smells good," I complimented.

"Thank you," she simpered.

While she rubbed my beard, she stared into my eyes, and that shit was mesmerizing as hell. Shit had me in a trance and before I knew it, I was kissing her lips. I expected her to pull back, but she didn't, so I deepened it.

"Mhmm," she moaned, making my dick jump. I detached my mouth from her lips and pressed them against her neck before I sucked on it lightly. Her damn kiss tasted better than any fuckin' Tootsie Roll ever made. Leaning up, I looked in her eyes and wrapped her legs around my waist and walked her back into the bedroom and laid her on the bed.

"I know you said we wouldn't have sex before we got married, but I need you in some form, baby. This shit is driving me crazy. I'm not going to penetrate you, but you got to let me taste you," I damn near begged. She looked like she was going to pass out just from me mentioning it, so I brought my lips back to hers.

"You trust me, Promise?" I asked.

"Yes," she breathed out.

"Good, now lie back for me."

I waited until she got herself positioned and lay back while I slipped her shorts and panties off.

"Damn," I groaned, staring down at her hairless, fat, and

juicy pussy. I couldn't even play with myself by staring. I needed to taste her, and I did just that. As soon as I swiped my tongue between her folds, she jumped.

"Calm down for me, baby. It's just my tongue. See." I stuck my tongue out and flicked her now protruding clit while she watched me. After a few more flicks of my tongue, I sucked her clit into my mouth and starting sucking like a breastfeeding baby.

"Ughn," she moaned, arching her back off the bed a little bit.

I sucked and bit on her clit until I felt her juices leaking and her legs started to tremble.

"Kna...Knasim. Oh...gah...what the fuck are you doing to me?" she whined.

"You're about to cum, baby, and I'm gon' need you to not hold that shit either. I feel that pussy pulsing, baby."

Her body started jerking, so I switched positions and fucked her with my tongue while I strummed her clit as she experienced her first orgasm.

"Ahh! Oh...my...shiiiit," she whimpered, humping my face as she rode the wave. I didn't let up until I felt like she was done, and she swatted my hand away. When I sat up and licked my lips, she was staring at me with a blank expression on her face.

"You good?" I asked.

"Yeah. That was intense," she admitted.

"Baby, that was just the beginning. Wait 'til I give you this dick," I smirked.

"Is it going to make me feel like that?"

"It's going to make you feel better," I responded cockily. I pecked her lips once more before I got up to go wash my face, but she grabbed my arm to stop me.

"Wassup?"

"Can you do what you just did again?" she asked shyly. Laughing, I kissed her lips, trailing my kisses down, nipping her nipples through her tank top before I made it back to her sweet pussy. I guess this was as close as I was going to get to consummating this shit, but I'd take it.

PROMISE Twelve

I woke up the next morning, still nestled in Knasim's arms. I thought it would be weird, but it was surprisingly welcoming. Besides him snoring occasionally, our first night was fine. I thought we were about to fight at one point though because he wanted to turn the TV off when he was about to go to sleep, and I told him I had to sleep with it on. He stared at me for about five minutes before he turned it back on. He acted as if he had an attitude with me, but that wore off quickly when he pulled me into his chest and wrapped his strong arms around me and kissed my forehead before calling me a scary cat because I was scared of the dark. I laughed because it was somewhat true. I wasn't scared of the dark, but I didn't want to be in complete darkness or silence. As soon as I was about to get up, his phone started ringing on the night-stand beside the bed. I don't know if he really didn't hear it or ignored it, but it was going off back to back.

"Knasim." I nudged him and called his name. He didn't move.

"Knasim," I said a little louder.

"Huh?" he answered groggily.

"Your phone is ringing." I tried to sit up, but he kept me locked in place as he leaned over and answered the phone.

"Hello?" I couldn't make it out the voice, but I knew it was a woman.

"Yeah, Ma. I told her. Yeah. Wait, I'll let you talk to her." He placed the phone on his chest. "She can hear you."

"Good morning, Promise. My son told me that you all talked about the engagement party and that you were okay with it. Do you have any plans for today?" his mother asked.

"Good morning, and no ma'am I don't."

"Great. Do you think you and your mother can meet with me at The Royale on Richmond Parkway?"

"Uh...I don't think that should be a problem. I'll call her to make sure she can make it and we'll meet you there," I said.

"Perfect," she said, excitedly. "It's a little after nine now. Will you be able to meet around three?" she asked.

"Uhm...yeah. That should be fine."

"Sounds like I'll see you then." She said goodbye to the both of us and hung up. Knasim picked his phone up and sat it back on the nightstand before trying to cuddle up against me.

"I know you heard your mama say she wanted us to meet her at three. I need to start getting ready. Plus, I got to pee." He sucked his teeth but eventually let me up.

After using the bathroom and washing my hands, I started my morning routine. When Knasim walked in, I was rinsing my mouth. Once he was done, I watched him walk to the sink to wash his hands and brush his teeth. He still hadn't said anything, and I was starting to wonder if last night was a mistake. That was until he rinsed his mouth and pulled me into his arms.

"Good morning, shorty," he greeted as he kissed my lips, then neck.

"Good morning. I thought you were about to start acting weird," I revealed.

"What made you think that?" he frowned.

"You came in here and didn't say anything."

"Shorty, I had to piss, and I'm still trying to wake up. You want me kissing on you with morning breath and shit?" he smirked.

"It's not like you haven't been blowing it in my face and neck all night," I joked. He mushed my head and started laughed.

"Get the fuck out of here," he laughed. "You going to clean this stuff off of my face?"

"All you have to do is wash it off and apply that oil to your face and beard," I instructed. He turned me around and pressed my back into the sink.

"But I like when you do it." The way he was staring into my eyes made me have flashbacks of last night.

"Okay," I simpered. He still didn't move.

"I need you to back up so I can get the stuff." After a few minutes, he finally backed up just a little so I could get the things I needed to clean his face. Since we did a full routine last night, all I needed to do this morning was clean that off.

I sat on the counter with him standing between my legs and repeated the process like I did last night. When I was done with him, I did mine and we headed downstairs to find something to eat because I was starving. I decided to call my mother to let her know about meeting Mrs. Richmond. I hope she will be able to make it. If not, I'd be fine.

"Good morning, Mommy."

"Good morning, baby. Is everything okay?" she asked. I could hear the concern in her voice. She knew how I felt about this situation with Knasim in the beginning and I appreciated her for helping me through it.

"Yes, Mommy. Everything is okay. I'm actually calling to see if you had any plans today."

"Girl, I'm stuck in this town with nothing to do. It's only so much shopping a girl can do." She laughed.

"You're absolutely right, but I never thought I'd hear you say that. But Mrs. Richmond wanted to meet today and go over things for an engagement party. Can you go?" I asked.

"Of course! See, this is another reason for me to shop." I could hear the smile in her voice and that, in turn, made me smile.

"It's not like you need a reason. She wants to meet at three. Is that good for you?"

"It sure is. Where do I need to meet y'all?"

"I can come pick you up," I offered.

"You don't have to do that. I can drive myself. Now, where are we going?" I gave my mother the information to the hotel, and she promised to meet me there at three. By the time I hung up, Knasim had already started cooking. When he heard me hang up, he turned his music on.

"Alexa, play Knas with a K's R&B station," he spoke. Tevin Campbell's "Tell Me What You Want Me To Do" crooned through the speaker.

"R&B lover?" I asked.

"Something like that. We got into a habit of cooking to this kind of music, so it stuck." he shrugged.

"And you cook, too?"

"I do. I'm no chef, but I can do a lil' something. Can you cook?" he asked.

"I can. I actually like cooking...baking, too."

"Oh yeah? So if I ask you to make me my favorite cake, you could do that?"

"Most likely. I'm obsessed with those baking shows, so I taught myself how to bake," I revealed.

"Like you did with your skin products?"

"Yep."

"I can dig it, shorty. You're fine, and a go-getter. I can fuck with it."

"I guess that's a compliment, so thank you."

"It was." I watched as he moved around the kitchen effortlessly with just his shorts on with the band of his briefs exposing the deep cut V that I had no business staring at.

"You keep looking at me like that and I'm going to show you just what to do wit' it," he smirked. My cheeks flushed with embarrassment because he had caught me lusting after him. Once he plated my bacon and eggs, he got a bowl of fruit and sat in on the table by us. We prayed and ate in silence for a few minutes until he broke the silence.

"Do you regret what happened last night?" he blurted out.

"No. Why did you ask me that?"

"I was just checking, shorty. I don't want you to think I'm pressuring you into no shit that you're not ready for."

"Didn't I ask you to do it again?" I simpered.

"Yeah, you did. I'm going to need you to hurry up and finish eating so I can do it again before you leave." The throbbing between my legs couldn't go unnoticed. I know he knew his words affected me by the way I moved in my seat and by the smirk plastered on his face.

"You have a busy day today?" I asked, breaking the silence.

"I hope not. I got a few things to check on, and actual funeral business. There's a funeral tomorrow at the home in The Heights. I just need to make sure that they covered everything."

"You need me to help?"

"Nah. Not there, anyway."

"Why not?"

"Because The Heights is not a place I want or need you to be. Ain't no telling when or if them niggas will start shooting. They don't give a fuck about it being a funeral. We never have females over there. They don't even work the legit side." I wasn't surprised at what he said because crime was everywhere. Cannon Hills had a similar area that I rarely frequented. Precious lived for shit like that, though.

"Have you been shot before?" I asked.

"Yep. Three times. The second time was the worst because it was in my chest. That shit felt like somebody sat a ton of bricks on my fuckin' chest. That was the longest recovery. The others were my shoulder both times." I was shocked, and a little turned on at the fact that he talked about getting shot so causally.

"Is that why you have inhalers?" I saw it with the stuff that Knicole brought over.

"Yeah. It's also the reason I don't smoke. I used to, but when I tried after getting shot and that shit burned worse than the actual wound and the cough was unbearable. I said fuck that shit."

"Makes sense. Does me burning the candles bother you?"

"Nah. I walked in here last night and that shit felt all cozy and shit. Felt like...home." He stared at me for a few minutes before getting up and grabbing me up in the process.

"What are you doing?" I giggled. He had me wrapped around his waist and headed upstairs.

"I couldn't sit there any longer and watch your nipples pressed up against that thin ass shirt you got on and not do shit about it. I'm about to get my fix, then you can get ready to leave," he said as he entered the room and dropped me on the bed. If he kept this up, he wouldn't have to wait for the wedding.

———

I finally got Knasim to leave me alone so I could get ready to meet our mothers. I was thankful that his brother Knight was blowing him up. By the time I pulled up to the hotel, it was 3:15. I didn't take into account of the traffic and Knasim didn't warn me. I walked inside and went to the restaurant where Mrs. Richmond told me they would be. When I got inside, I saw her and my mother sitting at a table along with Knicole, Denver, and another woman I didn't know.

"There she is," Mrs. Richmond announced. "You look gorgeous, Promise. Your skin is practically glowing," she observed.

"She makes her own skin care products," my mother mentioned.

"That ain't no skin regimen," Knicole blurted, causing Denver to laugh.

"Knicole!" her mother chastised.

"Hey, boo. I see we meet again," Denver spoke.

"I see."

"This is Syrena. Knasim's aunt, and Denver's mother-in-law," Mrs. Richmond introduced.

"It's nice to meet you. Have y'all been here long?"

"Not really. We had an appetizer and, of course, a drink while we waited. Are you ready to go see the ballroom?" she asked.

"Sure." We all got up and headed in the direction I assumed the ballroom was located. When we got inside, there was a guy inside that favored Knasim.

"Ladies, I see you made it," he said, walking over. He went to kiss Mrs. Syrena on her temple and then stepped to Denver.

"Denver, let me talk to you for a second," he said.

"I'm working, Kyandri," she sassed.

"Baby, it'll only take a minute," he said. Reluctantly, she excused herself and followed him.

"Those two work my last nerve," Mrs. Syrena said, shaking her head.

"They can't be any worse than Knight and Teyana," Knasim's mother said.

"Nobody's worse than Teyana," Knicole said.

"So, Knasim is the only single one?" I asked.

"Was," his mother said. "He *was* the only single one. Did you forget that the two of you are about to get married?" she smirked.

"Girl, Denver and Kyandri are like one of those celebrity

couples that you see together today, and tomorrow the blogs will be reporting they broke up. Chy, Kyan's wife, is a mess too, but you'll find out more about her later." Knicole was just telling all these people's business, and I was soaking it up.

"Who is Kyan?"

"That's my other son. He and Kyandri are twins," Mrs. Syrena revealed. I looked over at Denver and Kyandri, and she was blushing and rolling her eyes at the same time. She turned to walk off from him and he stopped her and engaged in a deep kiss.

"Damn, Ky. We ain't come here for all that!" Knicole yelled. The two lovebirds broke their kiss, and Kyandri slapped Denver on her butt as she sashayed off.

"Mind yo' business, Knic," he said. "I'm sorry for being rude. I'm Kyandri. Knasim's cousin. It's nice to finally meet you," he introduced his self.

"Nice to meet you too," I shook his hand that he held out. Mrs. Richmond introduced him to my mother and after he told us he would be around if he needed anything, he left us in the immaculate ballroom.

"Okay, now that the pest is gone. Let's get to work," Denver announced.

"Don't play my cousin, Denver," Knicole said. We all shared a laugh when Mrs. Richmond threatened to tie her lips together.

Denver walked us through every inch of the ballroom, going over the ideas that she came up with. You could tell that she was in her element because her words flowed effortlessly. I saw her work firsthand, so whatever she suggested, I was going with.

"So, Promise. I think that it would be a good idea if you and Knasim's favorite colors were incorporated. I already know his is black, and your mother told me yours was brown. I'm thinking black, gold, and champagne to soften the boldness of the two colors. What you think?" Denver asked.

"I like it. I trust your judgement."

"Perfect. I have a little over two weeks to pull this off, which is nothing. I'll set up a few meeting for us to get together on some things. I know I'm just decorating, but I got to make sure you have a bad ass dress. I have a homegirl that is a designer. I'm going to call her as soon as I leave here. When she tells me a day and time, I'll shoot you a text." Damn, was she going to breathe? I thought.

"Okay, I guess," I giggled.

Denver left, and we all started filing out. Knicole stopped me and asked if I wanted to go to a late lunch without the 'aunties' as she called them, and I agreed. I told my mother that I would probably come by tomorrow and we said our goodbyes.

"Ooh, you must've really put it on my brother if he let you drive his Benz. He acts like nobody can drive this car but him," Knicole said. I could tell she was being funny and not jealous like Precious would've been.

"I haven't done anything with your brother, Knicole. I admired the car and he let me drive it." I shrugged.

"Y'all did something," she insisted. Just as I was about to respond, Knasim's name flashed over the screen of the dashboard.

"Hello?" I answered.

"Wassup? Everything went okay?" he asked.

"Yeah. Denver is going to call me in a few days to go over a few details. She said something about her friend doing a dress for me, too."

"She must be talking about Jacie. She's straight," he replied.

"How did you know I had left already? You tracking me?" I asked.

"You must've forgotten I got eyes on you, baby. But nah, Trig called me when y'all left."

"Who?"

"My bad. Kyandri. He called and told me that y'all had everything squared away."

"Oh, ok." We were silent for a few seconds before Knicole put her two cents in.

"Y'all awkward as fuck," she laughed. "Knas, you just going to sit and listen to the girl breathe?"

"Man, Knic. The fuck you doing, bruh? Where y'all going?" he asked.

"I'm about to get Promise to drop me off to see my nigga," she said.

"Knic, don't get you, Promise, and that nigga fucked up. Stop playing wit' me for real." I could hear the agitation in his voice, and I thought it was cute.

"What I do?" I asked innocently.

"Don't play wit' me Promise. Yo' pussy still fresh on my breath, so the fuck you going around another nigga for?" he snarled.

"I knew it!" Knicole laughed. I wanted to die because I knew his ass didn't just put my business out there like that.

"Shut up, Knic," he snapped. I couldn't control my laughter because between the two of them, they had me rolling.

"Knasim, you didn't have to say all that, and we're going to a late lunch."

"Aight. Don't let Knicole get you fucked up," he said.

"Boy, shut up and bye!" She hung up in his face and I died laughing.

"Why did you do that?"

"Because he's annoying."

The phone started ringing again, and I answered right away.

"Knic, stop playing wit' me. I'm gon' knock yo' shit loose when I see yo' ass. Promise I'll be home a little late, but I'll call you."

"Okay." We said our goodbyes and hung up. I glanced over at Knicole, and she was grinning wide as hell.

"Spill it, bitch."

"What? There's nothing to spill," I lied.

"Lies. My brother just said his breath smells like your coochie, so something happened. I want to know what. Just don't tell me shit about my brother's dick." She made a face and shivered like she was disgusted.

"Trust me, I know nothing about your brother's dick. We didn't have sex. He just went down on me," I shrugged.

"That's it?"

"Yeah, that's it? Why did you say it like that?"

"Girl, I know you're a virgin," she blabbed.

"He told you that?"

"No. Knight did. Me and my brother's are close." She shrugged.

I didn't know how I felt about them discussing my private

business amongst themselves. Maybe I didn't understand because me and my sister weren't close.

"Don't look like that. Knas probably doesn't even know Knight told me. It's nothing to be ashamed of. I'm one too. We can form our own support group," she said, making me almost run off the road.

"Girl, what the fuck?" I cackled. "A support group? Please don't say that to nobody else," I continued to laugh.

"Hell, with the way my brothers and cousins act, I'll never lose it. It sucks being the only girl," she pouted, and I felt bad for her.

"They're hard on you, huh?"

"Hell yeah. Kyandri and Kyan aren't even my brothers, but you can't tell them that. Any time I get a boyfriend, it doesn't last long because they threaten him. I don't even get close to females anymore because they were using me too to get to my brothers. Teyana was my friend, and she started messing with Knight and because I wouldn't take her side in their bullshit, she stopped talking to me, too. I can't wait until she has that baby so I can beat her ass for playing with my brother," she rambled on.

"Knight has a baby on the way?"

"That's what she says. I'on believe her though because like I said, I was her friend and I know she's a hoe." She shrugged.

By the time we pulled up to the restaurant, I was full of all the tea that Knicole had dropped on me. This family gets interesting by the day.

PROMISE *Thirteen*

L unch with Knicole was refreshing. I never did stuff like this with Precious. She was always too busy with her friends to think about me. It also made me miss Kim. So when I got home, I called her.

"Hey, boo," she when she answered the phone.

"What you doing?" I asked.

"Nothing. I just got home not too long ago from getting my hair braided."

"I miss you, friend." I pouted.

"Aww...Friend I miss you too," she said.

"Pack a bag for a few weeks. This engagement party is coming up and I need my best friend here with me." I know I said Knicole and Denver were cool, but I needed somebody I'm familiar with.

"You ain't said nothing but a word. Let me look up prices right quick."

"Let me know the cost, and I'll pay it," I offered.

"You don't have to do that, Promise."

"I know I don't, but I want to. Besides, Knasim gave me this credit card and I rarely use it. Let me take care of everything."

"Okay, First Lady," she joked. "Where is that fine ass fiancé at, anyway? You still letting that man only put his mouth on you?" Kim was my best friend, so I told her everything. When I told her that Knasim went down on me, she was excited, like it had happened to her. She told me that I needed to test the waters, but I didn't think I was ready for all that just yet.

"There's a flight leaving out at nine in the morning. With the hour layover, I should get there around two," she said.

"That's perfect. I'll make sure I have one of the guest rooms ready for you. I can't wait to see you," I squealed.

"Me either, girl. I can't wait to come out there and see what those Wood Haven men have to offer."

"Chile, that's if Precious left any left for you to choose from. I'm pretty sure she's run through half of the population by now," I huffed.

"Have you seen or heard from her again?"

"Nope. I hadn't heard from her since the day I came home with the truck Knasim brought me. I don't even care if she shows up to the engagement party or not."

"You're inviting her?" she asked.

"It's an open invitation, and she's my sister."

"And she fucked your nigga before you did. Fuck her." Kim never liked Precious and vice versa. Kim said Precious was jealous of me and Precious said Kim was jealous of her. I tried to stay out of it as much as possible.

"I try not to think about that. So for my sanity, could you not bring it up?"

"I got you, boo, and I'm sorry. I just can't stand the way that she tries to come for you like it's your fault she has a loose coochie." I choked on my juice because this girl was crazy as hell.

"That's her issue, not mine, but fuck her. I can't wait until you get here. I haven't really been out and that'll give us something to do."

"You know I'm down for a good party."

We stayed on the phone for about two hours before we hung up. Knasim didn't come in until around ten. I was in the basement bottling up some products when he swaggered into the room shirtless with only a pair of cotton shorts on with socks and slides.

"Hey," I greeted.

"Wassup? How long you been down here?" he asked, walking up to me and kissing my neck.

"About an hour and a half," I replied. I noticed the way he was staring at me. His eyes were filled with pure lust, and it had my body tingling.

"You always walk around like this?" He gripped my butt and gave it a squeeze.

"For the most part, yeah. I like to be comfortable at home." I was currently in a sports bra and a pair of spandex shorts.

"You did that shit with your pops in the house?" he asked, with his brows knitted together.

"Yeah, why not? My daddy isn't some creep. Now, I didn't wear the short shorts when he was there." He just looked at me before placing his eyes on what I was doing.

"What's this?" he asked.

"It's a growth stimulating shampoo."

"Oh yeah? You think it'll help my edges?" he joked.

"Boy!" I laughed. "Oh, I talked to my best friend today, and she's coming into town tomorrow for a few weeks, if that's okay with you," I revealed.

"You already made the plans, right?"

"Yeah, but if it's a problem, I'll tell her to wait."

"Shorty, chill. It's cool. I saw the charge when you bought the ticket. I didn't see a charge for a hotel room, so I'm going to assume she's staying here?"

"Yeah, if you don't mind."

"Is she anything like your sister?" he quizzed, causing me to laugh.

"No, and please don't let her hear you say that. She can't stand Precious."

"Shit, you should've led wit' that. You need me to get anything ready for sis?" he asked.

"Sis?"

"Hell yeah. Anybody that hates Precious' raggedy hoe ass is a sister of mine." he smirked.

"You play too much," I laughed.

"I'm about to go upstairs and eat. I brought some shit from this soul food spot. It's enough so you can come up and eat when you're done." He kissed my lips and left me alone so I could finish the project I had started. I wasn't thinking about food until he said something, so I needed to hurry up.

I got up the next morning to Knasim, already gone. It kind of bothered me that he left without saying anything. His leaving wasn't what bothered me, but his occupation wasn't the best, so I did at least want to know he was leaving. When I got my hygiene out of the way, I called his phone.

"Wassup, shorty?" he answered.

"When did you leave?"

"Around six," he responded. "Why?"

"Can you tell me when you leave?" The line went silent. "Knasim?"

"Yeah, I'm here," he replied.

"I know what you're thinking, and that's not what this is. It's just that I don't want to not know where you're at or what's going on just in case. You know?" The line was still silent, but I knew he was still on the phone because I heard him breathing.

"You're right. My bad. I'm just not used to checking in or running my moves by anybody. I'll work on that."

"Thank you."

"You got everything straight for your friend, though?"

"Yeah. I just need to get myself together so I can go pick her up. We'll probably stop by my parent's house before we make our way back here."

"Sounds like a plan. I'll probably be back by the time y'all make it in, so we'll all go out tonight and welcome sis to town properly," he said.

"She'll love that. Thank you."

"It's no big deal, but let me go before I slap the shit out of Knight for calling my damn name so much." I laughed and hung up.

Once I got the guest bedroom situated for Kim, I got myself together so I could head out to the airport. I was leaving early because I was excited, and I didn't want to be late because Wood Haven's traffic was crazy as hell. When I got to the airport, I only waited for forty-five minutes before I saw Kim coming through the gate's terminal.

"Friiiieeennd!" she squealed when she saw me. I ran to her like I hadn't seen her in years.

"I missed you so much. Come on. I don't want to waste any time at this airport. I got my friend with me, and I can finally turn up," I cheered.

"Well, let's go."

I helped her load her bags into the back of my truck. I wanted to drive Knasim's Mercedes, but I didn't know how much stuff she would have, and I didn't want to risk having to put anything on his back seats.

"Bitch, this truck is niiice. The pictures and videos you sent did it no justice. Knasim got a brother? Hell, I'll arrange to marry his ass if I can get this kind of treatment," she voiced.

"Yeah, he has a brother, but he has a baby mama and from what I gathered, they're toxic as hell." I've only been around Knight twice, but I could tell that he was a live wire, so I can only imagine how his baby mama is.

"Ooh, thanks for the heads up. I'm not here for drama unless it involves me dragging Precious' ass. That I'll make time for." I laughed because I knew she meant every word, but I didn't want it to come to that.

"Chy, I'm not thinking about Precious. She wants me to kiss her ass and I'm not. I didn't do shit to her, so I'm cool on her ass. It's not like we were close, anyway." I shrugged.

"You're right, but I still won't hesitate to clock her ass if need be," she stated matter-of-factly.

We rode the short distance to a restaurant where we had lunch before we headed to my parent's house. We got there, and of course, my mother was the only one home.

"Well, look who it is? I knew you couldn't stay away too long," my mother greeted Kim what a hug.

"You know I couldn't stay away from my girl too long," Kim said. We followed my mother into the living room and talked with her for about two hours before we decided to leave, but not before promising to have lunch with her.

"I know you're staying long enough for the engagement party?" My mother asked.

"I sure am. I wouldn't miss this for the world," Kim replied.

After about an hour of catching up with my mother, Kim and I left so we could head back to the house so she could get settled. I told her that Knasim was taking us out later and that's all she needed to hear. When we pulled up to the gate, I thought she was going to lose her mind. The house we had in Cannon Hills was nice, but it still didn't have anything on this one.

"Bitch, is this all one house?" She asked as we pulled through the gate of the home I shared with Knasim.

"Yes...it's just one house. Too much house if you ask me, but that none of my business," I responded.

"Girl, hush. All of this is your business, so be quiet." All I did was shake my head at Kim because she would keep going like she knew everything she said was right. Pulling into the garage, I saw Knasim's Escalade parked in the spot that was vacant when I left, letting me know that he was inside. Kim and I got out and came through the garage door that led into the house. When we were inside, Knasim was inside the kitchen, closing the refrigerator.

"Wassup, y'all," he spoke.

"Hey," we both responded.

"Knasim, this is my best friend, Kim. Kim, this is Knasim," I introduced the two.

"Nice to meet you, Kim."

"Nice to finally meet you, too. I've heard a lot about you," she smirked, causing him to look at me and chuckle.

"I promise I'm not as bad as she has made me out to be," he grinned.

"Whatever. Let me show you where your room is so we can get you settled in."

I took Kim to her room, that was already downstairs. That way, if she got too drunk, she wouldn't have far to go.

"I'll take those bags since you didn't call me out to come get them," Knasim said.

"It wasn't a lot, so I didn't see why I had to call you," I responded.

"Promise, what did we talk about?" he asked, like he was annoyed. I didn't respond.

"Oop, friend. I guess he told you," Kim laughed.

"Shut up. You're supposed to be on my side." I playfully rolled my eyes at the both of them. Knasim came behind me and slapped me on the butt before heading toward the downstairs guest book.

"Bitch, you need to suck his dick or something. That man is fine as all hell, and he's a gentleman. You better stop playing," Kim whispered. Thank God Knasim didn't hear her ass. I waited until he walked out of the room before I continued the conversation.

"You think he'll step out if I don't?"

"I'm not saying that, but I'm pretty sure eating your

coochie ain't that damn satisfying. That man needs intimacy and a release, too."

"I'm pretty sure he's handling that," I countered.

"And what about the intimacy? I know you told me he agreed to be faithful, and I'm not saying he'd go out and do some dumb shit, but these niggas are weak and even dumber. Y'all may have come together unconventionally but y'all have potential. I'm not telling you to go and lose your virginity but find a way to please him just as much as he does you." I sat on the bed and thought about what she said and gave it some consideration. I would give what she said some thought, but it wasn't like I was about to walk up to him and ask could I suck it. I stayed downstairs with Kim to help her put her things away and show her where everything was. I even gave her a tour of the house and she was fascinated with everything and surprised that I did all the decorating. Well, technically Denver did, but I told her my vision and she went with it. She decided to take a nap since she was up early. By the time she got up, it would be time to get ready for our night out. When I left her room, I went upstairs to find something to wear. Walking into the bedroom I shared with Knasim was always nostalgic for me. This still didn't seem real, but my current living situation said otherwise.

Walling into my closet, I went to the clothes that I had hung up and thumbed through them to see what would catch my eye. My eyes landed on a pair of jeans that looked like cut-off shorts. They were cut off just below my butt cheeks and a flesh tone sheer fabric connected to the other half. The knees were frayed, and they stopped a little above my ankles. I found a sheer black off the shoulder crop top that I would pair with a white bra and heels. Satisfied with my selection. I left out of the closet and decided to take a nap myself so that I could be well rested for the night. I couldn't wait to get out...I needed it.

I woke up a few hours later to the sound of the shower running. That let me know Knasim was in there and I had to use the bathroom. I didn't want to invade his privacy, so I went to use the one that was in the hallway up here. When I came back, he was walking out of the bathroom with a towel wrapped around his waist and water droplets sprinkled on his chocolate skin. The smell of bergamot and papaya hit my nose.

"I see you finally woke up," he announced as he swaggered over to the dresser.

"Yeah, I had to use the bathroom, but I heard you in there, so I went to the one in the hallway."

"You didn't have to do that. Me taking a shower has nothing to do with you using the bathroom."

"I didn't want to invade your privacy," I stated.

"We're about to be married, shorty. Ain't no more privacy." He dropped his towel and stepped into his boxers as if I wasn't standing there. "See what I mean?" My words were still stuck in my throat, so I had to clear it before I spoke.

"Uhm...what time are we leaving?" I asked.

"Whenever y'all get ready. I know how long it can take women, so I'm on y'all time," he said.

"I'm not that bad. It didn't take me that long the last time."

"You didn't have your sidekick with you either," he smirked.

"Whatever. I'm about to go down and see if she's up, then I'm going to come back and start getting ready."

"Aight, shorty. I'll be dressed and out y'all way. Just let me know when y'all are ready." I nodded and headed downstairs to see if Kim was up yet. I knocked on the door and waited for her to open it. A few seconds later, I heard the lock turn and then it opened with her standing there in a t-shirt and sweats.

"Girl, what took you so long?" I asked.

"I didn't know if it was you or your man, and just in case it was him, I wanted to be presentable. I'm not Precious. I'm not about to be walking around him half naked and shit," she explained. I appreciated her for being respectful. I knew I didn't have to worry about her, especially since I knew Knasim would probably kick her out if she tried some shit.

"He's upstairs getting dressed. I came down here to see if you were up before I started getting ready myself."

"I'm about to start. You know what you're wearing yet?" she asked.

"Yeah. I picked it out before I took a nap. But bitch, why when I came from using the bathroom, Knasim was walking out of the one in our room with just his towel on," I revealed.

"And?"

"And he dropped his towel in front of me and I saw his dick," I whispered.

"That was the first time?"

"I mean...yeah. I've felt it before because we sleep in the same bed, but I never saw it. I lost all of my common sense when I saw that damn thing. Ain't no way in hell I'm letting that man inside of me with all that, and you talking about sucking it?" You would've thought that I told the funniest joke that she had ever heard by the way she was laughing. I didn't see a damn thing funny.

"What's so funny?"

"You bitch. You should see the look on your face. Oh my God, friend. I'm sorry, but that was funny."

"No, the hell it's not. I might be a virgin this whole damn marriage," I voiced.

"Promise, please. Stop being so damn dramatic. You'll be alright. But to ease you're mind; I'm going to teach you. Tomorrow we're going to the sex store and buy you one of those realistic dildos that you can practice on. By the time I'm done, Knasim will be thanking me. I'll be invited to all family functions after that," she laughed, and I joined in with her crazy ass. I left her and headed back upstairs. I passed Knasim coming from the bar area, and he looked good as fuck. He had on a black t-shirt with some kind of graphic printing on it. His lower half was covered in a pair of gray distressed jeans with what resembled black paint splashes on them. He had a pair of gray and black Jordan 1's on his feet. His jewelry was always simple, with only his Cuban Link chain and bracelet.

"She straight?" he asked.

"Yes. She's about to start getting ready and so am I," I informed him.

"Cool. Tell her she doesn't have to be locked up in the room all the time, either. She has access to everything in here, except my room," he said.

"What about me? Can I go in there?" He pulled me into his hard body.

"You can't take yo' lil' ass in there, either. You kicked me out of the basement, remember?" He gave my butt a squeeze before he smirked.

"I did not. You lie real bad." He laughed.

"If you say so. I'll be in there until y'all get ready."

"Okay."

"He kissed my lips and took his drink into his man cave while I headed upstairs to start getting ready."

The way he keeps touching and kissing me is making it harder and harder for me to keep my no sex rule intact.

I watched Promise saunter up the stairs and I couldn't take my eyes off of her fat ass jiggling in the little ass shorts she stayed wearing. I had to shake the filthy thoughts that were running rampant through my head. Once she was out of sight, I went to my man cave so I could chill out while the girls got dressed. As soon as I sat down and turned the TV to Sports Center, Knight was calling.

"Wassup, bruh?" I answered.

"Ain't shit. Y'all still coming out?" he asked. I mentioned to him earlier about Promise's homegirl coming into town and his ass was about to aggravate me to death about her ass.

"Yeah, nigga. I'm waiting for them to get ready."

"Bet. Since you got two females to wait on, I'll see your ass there because you won't be leaving no time soon," he said.

"I'm not even rushing them. That's why I got dressed and out the way. I'll hit you up when we're on the way."

"Bet."

I sat back and waited for the girls to get ready. After about an hour and a half, I got up to go see what the holdup was.

Promise was the first person I saw when I walked into the hallway. The outfit she had on had my feet stuck to the floor for a second.

"Damn," I mumbled. I walked over to her and pulled her to me, running my hand over her exposed skin.

"You look good, shorty. Too damn good," I admitted, and she blushed.

"Thank you," she replied.

"If I'm being honest, you're making this celibacy shit hard as fuck when you look the way that you do, shorty. You test my patience all day...every day. But don't stop." I leaned down and kissed her lips at the same time Kim was coming out of the room.

"Ok then. Y'all cute with the matching colors," she said. I looked down at Promise in her black top and gray jeans and smirked.

"Somebody has been looking in my closet, I see," she smirked back.

"Chill out. I was looking for you when I saw your outfit laid out, so I decided to match your fly. You don't want me looking like you, Promise?" I was now leaning down, towering over her. I could see her breathing pattern change by me being so close to her. I knew she could feel how hard my dick was. Kim talking broke us out of our trance.

"Y'all so cute, but can y'all do that and walk. I came to turn up. Not look at y'all drool over each other," she joked.

"You got that, sis." I nodded.

"Ooh, I'm sis now? Okay then, brother. Let's ride."

I went to get the truck and pulled in front of the door so they wouldn't have to walk through the garage. Tonight's vehicle of choice was my Mercedes-Maybach truck. I rarely brought this one out, but I figured tonight would be a good time to show it off. When the girls walked outside, I was already standing by the passenger side, waiting for them.

"Okay, brother. I see you how you rolling," Kim's crazy ass said. She was already alright in my book.

"Just a lil' light work. I figured I'd ride y'all around in style. I had both doors open, and while Kim got inside the back, I helped Promise into her seat. Leaning over, I fastened her seatbelt, then dropped a kiss on her lips before returning to my seat.

"Where are we going?" Promise asked.

"The Royal Room." I didn't frequent anything but my people's shit. Them other niggas were some haters, and I'd up my body count if I stepped foot in another establishment. Especially if I had Promise with me. I knew my lady was bad, and if I picked up on her innocence, them other niggas would too.

"That's the club connected to the hotel, right?" she asked.

"Yeah. My cousins are going to be there with their ladies, so you can meet them too. Well, you've already met Denver, but Kyan's wife, Aubree, will be with him," I informed.

"Any of these people single? Everybody you named sounds attached," Kim asked.

"My brother Knight is single," I replied.

"Don't he have a crazy ass baby mama? I don't do unnecessary drama," she said. I looked at her through the rearview, wondering how she knew that.

"Who told you that?" I saw her look at Promise and shook my head.

"I'm not even going to ask who told you. That messy shit has Knicole's ass all over it. But check it. He's single, so you don't have to worry about that. Teyana, on the other hand, is a live wire, so you might want to look out for her," I explained.

"She might want to look out for these hands because they don't discriminate," she stated, and I just shook my head. I drove the rest of the distance to the club, listening to them hold a conversation amongst themselves. When I pulled into the parking garage, Kim started her shit again.

"Okay, for the exclusive parking. Y'all keep it up and you won't be able to get rid of me," she said.

"You're more than welcome anytime you want," I assured. I got out to open her door then, Promise's. I helped her step down and pulled her close to me.

"I like your hair like this." She had it in its naturally curly and wild state and I loved that shit on her. I only saw it like this one time before.

"Thank you," she simpered.

I escorted the ladies inside the side entrance that was reserved for us. I noticed everybody's cars already here, so I knew we were the last ones to get here. When we got to the section, Knicole was the first person I saw.

"You talk too damn much," I fussed.

"Boy, what the hell are you talking about?"

"I'm not getting into all that. Just mind yo' business."

"Boy, fuck you. Ooh, Promise...you're cute boo," she said.

"Thank you. You do too," Promise responded.

"This is my best friend, Kim. Kim, this is Knasim's sister, Knicole." She introduced the two ladies before I escorted her over to where everybody was seated.

"'Bout time yo' ass showed up," Knight was the first to speak up.

"I'm here now, so shut the fuck up." I slapped hands with my brother before doing the same to my cousins and speaking to their ladies.

"Baby, you already met my brother and cousin, Kyandri and his lady. That's his brother, Kyan and his wife, Aubree." I introduced Promise and Aubree already had a stank ass look on her face.

"Nice to meet y'all," she spoke, and Kyan was the only one to say anything.

"Not tonight, Murda," was all I said. Aubree always showed her ass, and that nigga didn't care. I just knew shit wouldn't be good when they got home.

"Man," he drug out. "We'll see."

"And who do we have here?" Knight asked, like he didn't know.

"This is her homegirl, Kim."

"Wassup, Kim. It's nice to meet you, shorty," he flirted.

"I bet it is," she smirked.

We got settled in and as bad as I wanted Promise up under me; I let her do her thing with the girls. Well, all except Aubree's ass. She just sat off to the side, drinking like she had water in her cup.

"I see you're getting comfortable with your fiancée," Trig mentioned. When he brought Promise's name up, I unintentionally diverted my gaze to where she was. As if she felt me looking at her, she returned the gesture.

"You can say that. Shit, not bad as I thought it would be.

Especially since I can tolerate her ass." When I said that, Aubree started her shit.

"What is that supposed to mean, Knas? Are you insisting that Kyan only tolerates me?" she yelled. That caught the attention of the girls, and Knicole started.

"Aubree, don't get knocked on your drunk ass raising your voice at my brother. Take yo' drunk ass on somewhere wit' that bullshit before I help you sober up." It wasn't no need to try to calm Knicole down because one thing she didn't play about was her brothers and cousins.

"Kyan, so you're going to let them talk to me like that?" she yelled. He didn't even say anything. He nodded his head to one of the guards standing off to the side.

"Aye, take her home," he ordered.

"You're sending me home? Really Kyan? Your bitch must be here?" she yelled. Everybody watched in silence as she was escorted out and acting a damn fool.

"I apologize for that shit. As you can see, my wife is a lot to handle, and I don't have it in me tonight to deal with it. We're supposed to be celebrating, so let's turn up." I could feel him on that, but I felt bad for him as well. Aubree puts his ass through hell, and he just shrugs the shit off because she's his wife. Be we all knew; it was more to that story.

Everybody got back into their element after Aubree got escorted out. Promise looked so relaxed and carefree with her friend around. I know my people did what they needed to do to make her feel comfortable, but it wasn't nothing like having your own people around. I also noticed her taking back shots like it was water. I've never seen her drink like that, but then again, we've never been out before. I notice that they were heading out of the section and that made me call out to her.

"Promise, where y'all about to go?" I asked.

"To the bathroom," she answered. I wanted to object and tell her I'd escort her to Murda's office, but I didn't want to feel like I was smothering her.

"Damn, nigga. You gon' let the girl pee in peace," Knight joked.

"Shut the fuck up, and worry about Teyana's ass," I countered.

"I wish you would stop bringing that damn girl's name up. She gon' fuck round and pop up like Candy Man and I'm gon' beat yo' ass," he said.

"You ain't gon' do shit."

"Cuz, you looking comfortable wit' shorty. You on board with this whole marriage thing now?" Murda asked.

"I mean...she makes it easy. We just vibe and that's something I always wanted when I got married. She don't make a nigga's head hurt and shit, so I can deal with it."

"Shit, if we were all so lucky," he vented. I knew he had some shit going on with Aubree. Her only saving grace right now was their kids. I took a sip from my drink and thought about how much things could change with us within three years. I looked and noticed Denver come back into the section with Knicole. Promise and Kim were nowhere to be found.

"Where's Promise?" I asked.

"At the bar with Kim," Denver said. I didn't even waste my time getting up and heading in that direction.

"Knas, leave that damn girl alone," Knicole shouted, but I ignored her ass.

I took the stairs two at a time until I made it to the bottom. I had tunnel vision as I made my way to the bar and what I saw had me ready to snatch Promise's little ass up and the muthafucka that was showing them fake ass shiny teeth in her face. He definitely didn't know he was treading in dangerous territory.

"You keep turning me down like I'm an ugly nigga or something. Yo' nigga can't be all that if he let you out of his sight. Let me take care of you." I heard dude say, further pissing me the fuck off.

"The only thing that's going to be taken care of are your funeral arrangements and a fuckin' GoFundMe if you don't back the fuck up out my girl's face." Promise and Kim turned around at the sound of my voice. While Kim smirked, Promise's expression was neutral.

"Man, watch out. If she wanted me to lea—"

I cut his words off by knocking them shits back down his throat. He regained his stance, ready to swing, but the barrel of my Glock was staring him in the face.

"I see you're just as dumb as you look. Find the nearest exit before you be on a missing persons flyer. And that's me being nice." I smirked. The look in his eye let me know that he was pissed but knew better than to try his luck. He nodded his head and backed up with his hands in the air. Not even worrying about him doing shit, I turned my back and put my focus on Promise, who was still looking at me with that blank expression while I had a smile plastered on my face.

"Didn't I tell you the other day not to get you or these niggas fucked up, shorty? You thought I was playing?" I cocked my head to the side.

"He was just running his mouth. It wasn't like I was entertaining him." She shrugged.

"That don't make it no better. If you didn't want me to cut up, then you should've kept yo' pussy out of my mouth. Since you didn't, you got to deal with me cutting up on every nigga in yo' path that ain't me." I closed the space between us and peered down at her, waiting for her to object, but she never did. It was in her best interest that she didn't, anyway.

Time was winding down and by the time everybody was ready to go, all the girls were drunk as hell. Trig and Denver went to their suite over at the hotel, and so did Knicole. Knight helped me get Kim to the truck because it was no way in hell I would be able to get them both there at the same time. After dapping my brother up, I headed home. Thankfully, Kim was able to walk inside on her own, but I stayed close behind her just in case she stumbled. I was carrying Promise in my arms, so if she did fall wasn't too much I could do. I made sure she got inside her room before I trekked upstairs with Promise in my arms.

"I'm not that drunk, Knasim. I can walk," she voiced.

"That may be true, but I don't want to risk you falling. Let me do my job, shorty," I countered. Crossing the threshold of our bedroom, I sat her down on the bed so I could take off her shoes.

"So, I'm just a job to you?" She asked. I'm not going to lie her question caught me off guard.

"Huh?" I asked as a distraction.

"I asked you was I just a job to do. Is marrying me just a job so that you can inherit your spot in the organization. Is that all this is to you?" I didn't know how to answer her question, so I didn't. I didn't know what to say to that without saying the wrong thing. I'd be lying if I said that I haven't developed some sort of feelings for Promise, because I had. I didn't want to risk telling her my true feelings, and it was just the liquor talking for her.

"I'm not that drunk either, so I know what I'm saying. So, answer me," she demanded. Taking a deep breath and placing her foot back on the floor, I stood up and hovered over her.

"You think I would be doing all of this if this was just a job to me? Do you really think I would be trying to get to know you and care enough to spend my money on you? Not no chump change money either, Promise. I brought you a truck over a hundred thousand dollars. You think I did that shit for a tax write-off? Shorty, the only sexual thing between us is me eating your pussy, so you mean to tell me that I'm doing all that for a job, or because I love you?" I said the last part before I even knew it, shocking the shit out of both of us.

"You love me?" she whispered.

"Yeah, baby. I do. So, stop thinking this shit ain't real because it's as real as it gets." We held each other's gaze for the longest until she grabbed my face, pulling it to hers. The moment our lips connected; I felt a surge of energy that I never felt before. Shit was electrifying. I grabbed the back of her neck and pulled her deeper into the kiss, not stopping until she pushed me away. She sat up straight and reached for my belt buckle, but I stopped her.

"You don't have to do that, baby. I'm good. I promise."

"But I want to. You have no problem pleasuring me, so let me return the favor," she said.

I took another deep breath and closed my eyes. I felt her going at my belt again, and I again I stopped her.

"Baby, listen. I know you haven't done this shit before, so we can still wait. I told you it wasn't no pressure on my end."

"And I told you I wanted to do it. So let me. It can't be that hard." she shrugged and succeeded in pulling my mans out into her small hand. I was already leaking pre-cum and was anticipating the next move. Out of nowhere, Promise licked the tip like she was licking an ice cream cone and I damn near nutted on contact.

"Ssss," I hissed.

I looked down at her pretty face and she smiled at me before placing me in her mouth slowly.

"Tuck your teeth," I instructed, and she listened.

She kept moving her head up and down my dick like she was getting used to it.

"Keep doing what you're doing but let me feel your tongue, too," I commanded. I felt her tongue run down my shaft and I grabbed a hand full of her hair with both hands.

"Fuck, baby. Open ya mouth a lil' wider for me and relax your throat." I felt my nut rising that fast and I need to assist her.

When I felt her throat relax, I started stoking it, picking up my pace just a little.

Gawk

The sound of her gagging was like music to my ears.

"Shit, Promise. I'm about to nut," I groaned. When I said that, she fondled my balls and I think it caught both of us by surprise because I erupted down her throat, and she jumped at the motion.

"Fuuuck," I growled lowly as I emptied everything I had inside of me down her throat. When I was done, I flopped down on the bed beside her so I could catch my breath. I felt the bed dip, but I was too drained to move. Moments later, I heard the water running and her brushing her teeth. When she came back into the room, I jumped at the feeling of the warm towels she had to clean me off. I still didn't move because I didn't want my dick to get back hard.

She left to go put the washcloth in the hamper, and leaned over me when she got back and said, "I love you, too."

————

It's been a week since I told Promise I loved her and the same amount a time since she sucked my dick. To say I was shocked at my words and her actions were definitely an understatement. Once I got myself together. I tried to suck her pussy from its position in her body. I even asked her how she learned to suck dick and she told me she was watching videos to learn. She told me Kim offered to take her to get a plastic dick to practice on and all. Practice or not, my dick was the only one going inside of any hole in her body.

I left her and Kim to go meet Denver and the other ladies to finalize the details of the party. She also had to meet with the girl that was making her dress. I had a few meeting today, one being about Wood's ass. This nigga was acting like he was invisible and shit. First, the money at his house was looking shady, now the product that he was transporting was coming up short. Now, any other time, he would've been dead on the spot, but I had to start thinking more rationally now. He wasn't the only one on that route, so I needed to narrow it down. When I pulled up to the house in The Valley, everybody was there waiting.

"Nigga, get in house pussy and he's already being late. You ain't even hit yet and you're already wit' that sucker shit," Knight joked when I walked inside the basement.

"Mind yo' business. Don't you have a doctor's appointment or some shit to go to?" I snapped back. All he did was wave me off.

"Y'all just need to kill the nigga and get it over with," Murda voiced. His ass stayed ready to end somebody, and right now I felt him.

"In due time." I looked around the room and saw that Wood's ass wasn't even in attendance, so I turned my attention to the guys that worked that route with him.

"Where that nigga Wood at?" I asked. The only answer I got was shoulder shrugs and mumbles.

"None of y'all can talk now?" I cocked my head to the side.

"We don't know where that nigga at," a lil' nigga named Petey said.

"Ain't that yo' boy? How the fuck you don't know where he is?" Knight snapped.

"I don't know where he is because I don't be keeping up wit' another grown ass man," he stated with too much attitude.

"Aye, check it. Since you don't know where that nigga is, you can sit down until you do. Let that nigga know to stay from around my shit too," I ordered.

"The fuck, Knas! You can't just sit me down like that and I ain't do shit," he snapped.

"Nigga, I could kill you and you can lie down. The fuck you look like telling me what to do with my shit?" The look on his face let me know that he didn't like a single word that came out of my mouth, but knew he couldn't do shit about it.

"Now, like I was saying, none of y'all will have shit if I don't get this nigga. I don't play about my shit that belongs to me, but I do think I'm being fair by not killing all of y'all. I need the head of the houses to stay back, but the rest of y'all can leave," I ordered. Everyone filed out except the ones I asked to stay. When they left, Knight took over.

"Ok, so I'm going to send Chris out to change the security access on all the houses. The trucks will get new trackers as well. I don't know what the fuck this nigga is up to, but I don't need him thinking he can come and get more than he has. If he comes to any of the houses while y'all are there, call one of us, and we'll be on the way. Don't let the nigga think nothing is wrong, just call. If I hear he's been spotted at any house and I don't receive a call, I'm throwing all you niggas in the incinerator. We clear?"

"Yeah," they all voiced.

"Aight, bet. I'm done." We watched them leave, and I shook my head in frustration.

"I don't need this bullshit right now. I got too much going on to have to deal with this shit. I need to handle this like yesterday," I voiced.

"I agree," Trig said.

"We got this shit, bruh. Handle ya shit on the home front," Knight said.

"Yeah, I'm going to do that too, but I'm not about to give

Knox another reason to be on his bullshit." All I needed was one thing to be mishandled before I took over completely.

We all slapped hands and parted ways. I had to run by the house in The Bay to check on Thad's shipment. Trig offered to do it for me, but I needed to lay eyes on shit out there myself. I was serious when I said that he needed to tell Promise before I did.

Everything seemed to be into place once I got there, so I didn't stay long. I headed to my next stop and was glad that he was still there.

"Knasim, my friend. How are you doing today?" Kadeem greeted me as soon as I walked into the store. Kadeem was a jewelry that we've been using for years. His shit was flawless and always exceeded expectations. I knew he would have what I was looking for.

"Wassup. I need you to show me your engagement rings," I said, getting straight to the point.

"Engagement ring, huh? Who's the lucky lady?" he asked.

"None of your business. Do you have something for me or not?" He laughed and walked over to the display case that held rings. He pulled a tray out and started laying a few out.

"What's her style?" he asked.

"She's simple. She likes nice shit, but she isn't too flashy," I stated. I watched as he picked up three rings and handed them to me. None of them stuck out until I got to the last one.

"How much is this one?" I asked.

"Ahh...you have a good eye, my friend. This here beauty is eight carats total weight. As you can see, there are diamonds on the band as well. The princess cut halo is elegant enough to where your lady will fall in love with you all over again once she lays her eyes on it," he said, still not answering my question.

"You still not answering my question, Kadeem. How much is it?"

"For you...I'll let it go for two hundred."

Damn, two hundred stacks was a lot for an engagemnt ring, but Promise deserved it, and this shit was nice.

"Aight. Clean my shit up and box it real nice for me. You got any ladies' Cuban Link's in?"

"I actually got some new ones in today. Let me show you." I followed Kadeem to another case and allowed him to show me the chains he got in. After it was said and done, I spent a cool mil on Promise, and I didn't even know how the pussy felt. Love was definitely a muthafucka.

PROMISE Thirteen

The day of the party had finally arrived, and it was like I was just realizing how real this was. The night Knasim told me he loved me opened up a set of emotions that I never knew I possessed. I knew I had feelings for him, but in the back of my mind I couldn't help to think he was only doing this to fulfill his position within The RCF. I know I was dead against this arrangement from the beginning, but when you're forced into a situation; you have to make the best of it. I can't complain and say that I wasn't enjoying the position I was forced into because Knasim made it more than pleasurable.

All the women, minus Precious and Aubree, were now in Denver's suite at the hotel where Knasim had a glam squad sent to help us get ready. The room was decked out with champagne and charcuterie boards for us to have something to snack on.

"So, Promise. Are you excited yet?" Denver asked.

"Kind of. I'm still nervous, but Knasim makes all of this easy to go along with," I admitted.

"I'm glad to hear that, sweetie. I know this may not have been what you thought your future would look like, but you are the perfect pick for my son. No offense, Lydia," Mrs. Richmond said.

"None taken," my mother replied.

"Have you heard from Precious?" I asked my mother.

"No. I did call her, but she didn't respond."

"She didn't reply to my text either," I revealed.

"I don't know why you texted her in the first place. Let her stay where she's at," Kim fussed.

"She's still my sister," I countered. "The last thing I need is for her to have another reason to start with me."

"Girl, fuck yo' sister," Knicole voiced.

"Knicole!" Mrs. Richmond chastised, and Knicole shrugged.

"I'm just saying. The three of us are more her sisters than the one she got."

"Facts," Kim co-signed.

"Can we stop talking about Precious for now? I don't that negative energy on me tonight."

"You're right, sweetheart. Let's get you all dolled up and ready to shine on your fiancé's arm tonight," my mother stated.

"Baby, Jacie did her thing with your dress. Knasim might not let you out of his sight," Denver chimed in.

"Chy, he doesn't now. You should see them at the house. They're like Siamese twins, but it's so cute," Kim said, causing me to blush. We were already building our connection and initiating intimacy, but after we said, 'I love you', he had turned it up a notch.

The mother's left to go to their prospective suites, leaving the four of us in Denver's. Since we took over, Kyandri took his things down to Knasim's room, where all the other men were. It was Denver's idea that everyone was already at the hotel so that we would be in a central location.

I was slipping on my shoes when Knasim walked through the door of the room. When I saw him dressed in his tux, my panties instantly got soaked. He never dressed up, but he did for the occasion, and I wasn't disappointed at all. His cream-colored jacket had gold designs all over and fit perfectly. The cream-colored shirt he wore underneath was unbuttoned, exposing the Cuban Link that he always wore around his neck. The black slacks were tailored to perfection and the Ferragamo dress shoes were the perfect way to complement the outfit.

"Damn," he said as soon as he entered the room. Kim was helping me zip my dress up but excused herself as soon as Knasim came in.

"You look...shit...I can't even explain it," he voiced, swaggering closer to me.

"You don't look too bad yourself. I like this look on you. You clean up pretty nice."

"You know I do what I do," he smirked, popping his collar.

"Are you about ready?" he asked.

"Yes. I just need to put my accessories on."

"Let me help you with that?" He pulled out two boxes that I didn't notice when he first walked in.

"What's this?" I asked.

"It's an engagement gift." I took the box out of his hand and when I opened it, my mouth hit the floor.

"Knasim, this is beautiful," I cooed.

In the box was a stunning Cuban Link necklace and matching bracelet. The set was a more feminine version of the one he wore.

"Just a lil' something. Here, let me put it on you." I handed him the box, and he removed both of the pieces before he clasped them on my neck and right wrist. Standing behind me in the mirror, I admired how good we looked.

"Now you almost look like the First Lady," he smirked.

"Almost, huh?"

"Yeah. You need this to finish the look." He pulled a blue velvet ring box out of his pocket and opened it to reveal the prettiest ring I had ever seen.

"Knasim..." I trailed off.

"This shit wouldn't be complete without a ring. Our thirty days are officially over tomorrow, but we're already sixty days in. If you accept this ring, then I promise I'll spend the rest of my life loving you and treating you better than any nigga walking the face of this Earth could. If you reject it, I'll go downstairs right now and tell everybody to go home, and we can call this whole thing off." I looked into his eyes to see if I could see any sincerity in them and that's all I saw, along with the love that he had for me. These past two months I found myself falling for Knasim and I wouldn't want anything more than to have him be the one who loves me for the rest of my life.

Instead of answering, I stuck my left hand out and waited for him to slide the ring on my finger. The smirk on his face let me know that he was happy with my decision, and he slid the ring on my finger. It was gorgeous and not over the top.

"You really want to do this, shorty?" he asked.

"I do," I simpered. My response warranted him to pull me close to his body and kiss my lips with enough passion to last a lifetime. We didn't break apart until someone started banging on the door.

"Bring y'all asses on. Whatever y'all doing can wait until afterward." That was Knight. While I laughed, Knasim looked angry.

"I'm gon' beat this nigga's ass," he fussed.

"Come on. We don't want to be late to our own party," I voiced.

Taking my hand, he escorted me out of the room where everybody was dressed and waiting. Knicole was the first one to see my ring and comment.

"Gah damn, Promise! My brother iced you the fuck out," she said.

"Damn, nigga. Did Kadeem have anything left?" Kyandri asked.

"I left y'all a lil' something. I had to get my baby right for tonight," he boasted.

"Damn, bruh. You spending like this? Let me get twenty dollars," Kim joked, making everybody laugh, even Aubree. She looked to be in a better mood tonight.

Everyone filed out of the room and while they went one way, Knasim and I went another. The ballroom had two levels, and we were going to present ourselves from the upper level and ride the glass elevator down to the main floor.

"You ready to do this?" he asked, looking down at me.

"I am." He held my hand and walked out the side door as

our names were being announced. I felt like royalty waving at my loyal subjects. Knasim waved at a few before we got on the elevator and made our way to the main floor.

"You know I'm gon' eat yo' pussy real good when we leave here, right?" he said into my neck as we rode the way down. He didn't care that people could see us and at the moment, neither did I. When we stepped off, our parent's bombarded us to see my ring.

"Damn, Knic. You need some business," he playfully joked.

"Son, you did real good. I might need to ask your father for an upgrade," his mother said.

"I second that," my mother chimed in.

"I'm proud of you, son," I heard his father say as he gave him a hug.

"You look beautiful, baby girl," my father said, hugging me. When he let me go, I saw the look Knasim gave him. I wouldn't say anything now, but I would later.

Everything turned out nice. Denver really had an eye for decorating. I hope she knew how to multitask because I was going to ask her to be a bridesmaid, but I wanted her to decorate as well. I spent all night being introduced to different associates of Knasim's. I met the workers from the funeral homes, and I'm pretty sure most of them were from the illegal side. I was accepted immediately, and that made everything that much easier for me. It was time for Knasim to make his speech. He stood in front of the crowd while I stood off to the side. While he thanked our guest for coming out and celebrating with us until our nemesis arrived.

"Aww...that's so sweet. The man that was supposed to marry me is faking like he's so in love with my sister. Did you tell them that I was supposed to be his wife and not you?" Precious taunted. "Did you tell them that he was still fucking bitches because you're still a virgin?" I wanted to die, but I was going to kill her ass before I did.

"Bitch!" Kim yelled, heading in her direction before I could.

"Get the fuck off of me!" she yelled at the men, attempting to restrain her.

"Precious! What the hell is wrong with you?" our father asked angrily? "Have you lost your mind?"

"It's not like you care! Everything is always about your sweet and innocent Promise," she argued.

"Precious, that's enough!" our mother said.

"Get her the fuck out of here!" Knasim barked. I was so pissed I couldn't move. That was until the next sentence flowed through her lips.

"I bet she can't suck your dick like I can. I know you still think about it," she said with a sinister grin on her face. It only lasted a second though, because before she could put a period at the end of that statement, I was knocking it back down her throat. I tried to knock her teeth in her ass because I was tired of her playing with me. I tried to dislocate her head from her shoulders, but I felt a pair of strong arms wrapping around me and picking me up.

"Baby, let go," he spoke in my ear.

When they got us separated. They told her she needed to leave while she still had the chance.

"Aye, go bring my truck around," Knasim ordered.

"I'm so glad you knocked that bitch on her ass. I swear if you didn't I was," Kim voiced.

"No...we were," Knicole said.

"Baby, I'm sorry. I don't understand why she's going on like this, but me and your father are putting a stop to her shit tonight." My mother only cursed when she got pissed, so it was apparent that she was tired of Precious.

"You good?" Knasim asked. His tone did nothing to hide the anger on his face. While his voice was soothing, his face was nothing but.

"Yes. I'm fine."

"Aight. Let's get out of here."

We left out the front of the hotel. I saw Knasim's truck pulling up just as we were walking out the door. As soon as the driver's door came open, shots rang out.

"Get down!" I heard Knight yell. I was still behind Knasim, so he pushed me back inside and started shooting with his brother and cousin's. The shots finally subsided, and he came back inside and got me.

"You okay?" he asked, running his eyes over my body for any signs of injury.

"I...I'm fine. You're bleeding."

"It's a graze. Come on. We're riding with Knight. I need to get y'all home." He ushered us back toward the side entrance and back into the parking garage. I saw a few people that were said to be his workers wounded, even though he tried to shield that from me.

"Aye, y'all meet us at The Bay after you get them situated," he said to his cousins. Once we got to Knight's truck, he helped me inside the back while he climbed in beside me.

"Does it hurt?" I asked.

"Shit stings like a muthafucka. I'll take care of that later. I need to get you home and out of the way first." He pulled me close to his body and laid his head back on the seat with his eyes clothes. His heart was beating out of his chest, so I knew his adrenaline was still high. I locked my hands into his and laid my head on his shoulder. We weren't even married yet, and the drama was already starting.

Sixteen

My fuckin' shoulder was killing me, but I shook through that shit. I needed to keep a level head before I did more damage than I intended to. Promise had laid her head on my good shoulder, and I could tell that she was shaken up and that pissed me off more than getting shot. I would bet my life that nigga Wood was behind this shit. He better hope he has time to get right with his maker before I find his ass. Knight pulled up to my house and helped Kim out while I helped Promise.

"I'll meet you at The Bay when I'm done here. I'll call you when I'm on the way," I said to my brother as I stood in front my door.

"You know that nigga dying, right?" he grimaced.

"That nigga already dead," I retorted. "Put eyes on every fuckin' body that's close to him. I don't care if it's his third-grade teacher. Watch their ass too. I'll be there within the hour. I need to clean my fuckin' shoulder up and make sure Promise is straight," I said.

"Aight, I'll head that way now and wait on y'all niggas." We slapped hands, and I went to look for Kim first. I got to her room and knocked. When she opened the door, I glanced at her body only to see if I saw any physical signs of injury.

"You good?" I asked.

"Yeah. I'm fine. I scraped my knee when I fell, but other than that, I'm fine."

"Okay, good. My bad about this shit. I know you didn't come down here for that," I apologized.

"You don't need to apologize. I knew the risk and y'all made sure we were good. My friend is lucky to have you." I nodded and stuck my hand out to give her a pound before heading upstairs to check on Promise. When I got inside the room, didn't see her. That meant she was either in her closet or in the bathroom. I looked toward the bathroom, and it was dark so that left the closet. Stepping inside, I found her sliding her dress down her thick frame. When she saw me, she walked over to me with nothing but her thongs on. If I didn't have shit to go handle, I would've had my head buried between her legs by now. She carefully slid my jacket and shirt off before inspecting my wound.

"Come on," she instructed.

I followed her out of her closet and into the bathroom, where she went to the shelf in the small closet and retrieved a bottle of peroxide and the first aid kit. Once she had everything she needed, she moved to the shower and turned it on. All of this was done in silence. I observed her move around and when she took her thong off, I almost lost it.

"What are you doing?" I asked.

"About to clean you up. Get undressed."

"Promise," I groaned.

"Knasim," she countered.

Not wanting to keep going back and forth, I undressed my bottom half and walked over to the shower, allowing her to go ahead of me. I watched intently as she moved around the spacious shower, gathering my things.

"Sit on the bench," she ordered.

Once I sat down, she starting cleaning my wound with the wet washcloth.

"Ssss," I hissed.

"I'm sorry," she said, just above a whisper.

"You're good, baby," I assured.

She continued to clean me up and when I saw her pick up the peroxide bottle; I had to brace myself because I knew that shit was about to burn like a muthafucka. No sooner than the thought crossed my mind, she was pouring the liquid on my shoulder, making me groan out loud.

"Fuck!" I was gritting my teeth so hard I just knew I was about to break them. She must've poured the whole damn bottle on my shit because it felt like my damn arm was on fire.

"I'm almost done," she said.

After she cleaned it up, she told me to stand up while she washed me up before washing herself. When we got out, she wrapped a towel around my waist and then one around her body. I saw her hop on the counter and chuckled because she knew I wasn't about to sit on that little ass stool. I watched her as she dressed my wound and when she looked into my eyes; I saw just how much she loved me.

"I know what you're about to go do, so I'm not going to stop you. Just be careful and make it back to me in one piece."

Kissing her lips, I said, "I wouldn't have it any other way."

I pulled up to The Bay almost two hours later. As usual, they were already in place, but didn't give me much slack this time because they knew the effects of getting shot.

"Sis and her friend straight?" Knight asked once I entered the room.

"Yeah. Kim scraped her knee but other than that, she's good."

"Damn. I didn't mean to push her that hard. I just reacted. I need to make sure I apologize for that shit," he said.

"Your shoulder straight?" Trig asked.

"Yeah. Promise got me right. I think she low-key was punishing me for getting wounded because she poured the whole damn bottle of peroxide on my shit. I wanted to kick her lil' ass away from me." They all laughed, whereas I didn't find that shit funny.

"Fuck y'all. Everything ready to go?"

"Yep," they replied in unison.

"Well, let's ride." The four of us headed to the back out Escalade and piled inside. Me and Knight occupied the front while Trig and Murda held down the back. The first stop would be the house he shared with his baby mama, Raven. We knew they had two kids, so we were going to proceed with caution.

We pulled up on the street and cut the lights before we pulled into the driveway. Trig and Murda didn't even need instructions because they were already headed toward the back of the house. I didn't bother with knocking and kicking the door down because unbeknownst to either of them; I had keys to all the worker's houses. A muthafucka would never just slip out on me. When I opened the door, no alarm went off.

"Stupid ass nigga don't even have an alarm and his kids live here," Knight voiced, shaking his head while he went to the back to let our cousins in. While Murda went into the garage, I went up the stairs.

I went from room to room with my Glock leading the way but came up empty. Each time. I returned to the lower level, and they came up empty, too.

"This nigga probably already moved them," Murda said.

"Nah, it looks like nobody has been here, so her and the kids might be out of town or some shit. We'll just keep somebody on this muthafucka until she shows up." We left the house the same way that we came in. Our next spot was that nigga Petey's house. He was Wood's little flunky, so he knew something.

His spot was farther out back in The Heights. It didn't matter what time it was; it was always live over here. When we got out and headed up the gate that led to Petey's yard, I heard the whispers of the people standing by when I walked up. Letting myself inside like I did the previous time before, I walked inside and Petey wasn't in sight.

"Y'all go to the back while I check the rooms." Knight covered me as I walked through the house. A dark figure moving in the darkness of what looked like a dining room caught my eye, so I let off a shot.

"Ahh!" a male voice yelled out.

We all headed in the direction the voice came from with our guns drawn. Murda flipped the light on and this nigga Petey was rocking on the floor, holding his side. I walked closer to him and kicked him over onto her back.

"The fuck Wood at?" I asked.

"Fu...fuck you," he stuttered.

"Look, I don't have time for the theatrics. I know the lines. So skip all that bullshit and tell me what I want to know." I had my foot pressed down on his chest, barring him from getting up.

"I don...I don't know," he groaned.

"Aye, my boy. You gon' die anyway, but can you at least be useful before you do?" Trig asked, clearly annoyed. He was taking too long to respond, so I switched the pressure to his wound.

"Ahh! Man...fuuuck!" he groaned out in agony.

"Since you don't have shit to say, blame that nigga when you get to hell." I fired three shots in his chest and one in the center of his forehead."

"They're already on the way," Knight said.

"Bet. Let's go. My fuckin' shoulder hurtin' like a bitch. I need to take some meds and sleep this shit off. We'll resume this shit tomorrow." My head was thumping and so was my shoulder. I already lost a lot of blood, and I came out running around like Rambo.

Knight dropped me back home, and it was almost four in the morning, but Promise was still up.

"I didn't expect you to still be up."

"I couldn't sleep until you got back," she responded.

"I appreciate that, baby, but I don't want you losing sleep over me." I started to get undressed and winced at the spin.

That caused Promise to jump into action. She took her time pulling the shirt over my head and onto the floor.

"You're bleeding again," she stated.

"Yeah, I know. I'm about to hop in the shower. Can you take my clothes to the incinerator while I wash up?' She nodded and grabbed my clothes and shoes that I just discarded.

By the time I was done in the shower, Promise was just walking back into the room. I was already lying down with my good arm covering my eyes.

"I stayed and made sure everything burned down before I turned it back off," she said.

"'Preciate that, baby."

"Do you need anything for pain?"

"Nah. I have some Percs and antibiotics already. We have a doctor that makes sure we don't run out," I replied. "Come, lie down so I can get some rest." I watched her as she walked over to her side of the bed and got in. I thanked God I already slept closet to the door because I wouldn't be able to handle the pressure of her lying on my right side. I took the pills before I got into the shower, so they were already kicking in.

"Did you find him?" she asked.

"Nah, but he can't hide forever." She was quiet, like she was thinking.

"Everything is going to be fine, Promise."

"How can you be sure?" she asked.

"Have I ever lied to you?"

"No," she answered quickly.

"Then I'm not about to start." I kissed her forehead and pulled her closer to me as I started to drift off to sleep.

That nigga couldn't hide forever.

I was going to visit my parents today, and I hoped my father was home because I needed to know what that look was about between him and Knasim. I know he wasn't in his feelings now when all of this was his idea in the first place. When I got there, Kim and I got out and I let us in with my key. I found my mother in the living room reading a book. When she noticed me and Kim, she smiled and put it down.

"This is a nice surprise. What are you two up to?" she asked as we took a seat.

"Nothing much. I wanted to come check on y'all, especially after what happened at the engagement party." I saw the solemn look on my mother's face, and it made me want to bust Precious in her shit again.

"Promise, I'm sorry about Precious' outburst. I really thought that girl had gotten over it. I just hate to see my daughter's at odds when it's unnecessary. I blame your father and I because even though we raised y'all with the same morals and standards, she drifted away and instead of reeling her back in, we just let her do whatever she wanted because we were tired of repeating ourselves. With your father being gone most of the time, it was easier to let her do what she wanted rather than deal with a rebellious teen. That's a mistake that'll I'll own up to. When I lay eyes on her again, I'll probably lay my hands on her too. She knows I hate to be humiliated, and she brought that ghetto shit in there." Hearing my mother take blame for Precious' behavior made me feel some kind of way. Yes, she thought she created that monster, but Precious knew better. She just didn't give a fuck.

"It's not your fault. Precious is grown and knows what she's doing. Like you said, you did your best with the both of us and never treated us any differently. Everything she did, she chose because she wanted to. That has nothing to do with you and daddy," I assured.

"I know, baby. I can't help but feel responsible, though."

"Mrs. Lydia, none of that is on you. Everybody in this room knows how Precious is. She finally got what she deserved and if I lay eyes on her before I leave, I'm throwing these hands. Just thought I'd warn you," Kim voiced with a shrug of her shoulders.

"And I wouldn't be mad at all," my mother replied.

"Where's Daddy?" I asked.

"He's in his office." I nodded and headed toward my father's office. I knocked on the door and waited for him to grant my entrance before I walked inside. When I opened the door, he was seated behind his desk looking over some papers that were sprawled across his desk.

"Well, hey there, baby girl. What brings you by?" he asked, piling the papers and moving them out of the way. He stood up to give me a hug and kissed my temple before we both took our seats.

"I came to check on you and Mommy. Things got a little hectic at the engagement party, and I didn't get a chance to see you before I left."

"About that. Are you okay?" he asked.

"I'm fine. Knasim got grazed, and Kim scraped her knee. Other than that, everybody is okay."

"It's unfortunate that things went down like that. I hate that your sister came in there with her bullshit."

"I just talked to Mommy about that and I'm tired of talking about it. I'm more concerned with the look you and Knasim exchanged. What was that about?" I could see his demeanor change when I asked that question. It was like he wasn't expecting me to ask about it. Whether he expected it or not, I wasn't leaving until I got an answer.

"I didn't know you saw that. Well, if you're here asking me, then I guess Knasim hadn't told you anything yet."

"Tell me what?" I sat up and waited for my father to start talking. He finally cleared his throat and started speaking.

"I know I've kept you and your sister away from what I do for a living, and it was for good reason. It's not like it's from any reputable job, but it awarded you all with a lavish lifestyle that you had and still have. I know you remember Knox saying things didn't work out with my previous business partner. That was because I had to kill him for going against the grain. With him no longer amongst the living, that meant I had to find another courier for my business."

"And what business is that?" I asked.

"Uhm...well, baby girl. I traffic human organs," he revealed and to say I was shocked wouldn't begin to describe the emotions I was feeling at that very moment.

"Excuse me? You traffic human organs and you think that's okay?"

"It's not like how you're thinking, sweetheart. I don't go out and kill these people, but I have people that send me the organs after they have. I only service high end clients who need transplants and don't want to wait on lists for their family members. It may seem unethical, but it's a living." I sat back and looked at my father in disbelief. I didn't know if this was a good thing or not. I mean, he was doing something to help other families, but something just didn't sit right with me about it.

"So you mean to tell me you just have hearts and other functioning body organs just floating around. Daddy, that's sick."

"Call it what you want, Promise, but it's a living. A living that provided you with everything that you have. Even that business of yours that you take so much pride in. You're sitting here judging me and you're marrying a man that is about to be the head of an entire criminal organization. You have no room to judge me, baby girl." I looked at my father in disbelief. I couldn't believe he was being so nonchalant about this.

"The difference between you and Knasim is that he didn't lie to me about what he did. He was upfront and, if I remember correctly, you're the reason I'm marrying him in the first in place. Or did you forget?" I was livid that he tried to use me marrying Knasim against me. This was his idea in the first place. Granted, I was dead against it to begin with it, but I don't regret following through with it now.

"If that's what you want to think, then go ahead, but he's

no better than me." I was done with this conversation. I didn't even give him the respect of saying anything else. I just got up and left. When I got back to the living room, Kim and my mother were still sitting around talking.

"Kim, I'm ready," I announced when I made it back to them.

"Is everything okay, sweetheart?" my mother asked.

"Ask your husband," I said, picking up my purse.

"Promise, what's wrong?" she asked. I ignored her because I didn't want to talk to her either. I walked out with Kim following me and when we got inside the truck, she started with the questions.

"What's wrong?" she asked.

"My daddy just told me that he traffics human organs for a living."

"Are you serious?"

"Apparently. That's the business that he and The RCF have together." I was fuming and I guess it's because I was left in the dark about everything.

"Damn. It sounds crazy, but what are you really mad about? It's not like you didn't know he was into some illegal shit, and now you're marrying a whole cartel leader. What's the difference, Promise?" I didn't respond to her because I was too busy texting Knasim.

Me: I need you to meet me at the house.

Knasim: Baby I'm kind of busy right now. Can it wait?

Me: No it can not.

I knew I was being irrational, but I was upset.

Knasim: Aight...I'll be there in a few.

I put my phone down and drove to the house so that I could be there waiting on Knasim. I needed him to look me in my eyes when we talked. I didn't want to do none of this over the phone.

"Promise, I know you're not about to argue with that man about something that is on your daddy?" I didn't respond.

"Really, Promise? You can't be serious right now," she said.

"I'm not about to start with him but I think we need to talk."

"But you're upset, and he didn't do anything. You need to think about what you're going to say before you see him. I don't want you to tarnish y'all's relationship, especially after both of you admitted to being in love. Whatever your father did or is doing has nothing to do with Knasim." I heard her, but I still think we needed to sit down and talk.

KNASIM
Eighteen

I was in the middle of a meeting when Promise texted. I normally would never entertain my phone if I was in a meeting, but this wasn't just anyone. This was about to be my wife. I needed her to know that she would always be my top priority. When she requested that I come home and it couldn't wait, I got alarmed.

"Aye, I need to run by the house. Can you finish this?" I asked Knight. He nodded and asked me was everything okay, but I didn't have that answer for him. On the way out, I told him I would keep him posted. I wasted no time getting in my Range and pulling off. I made it to my house in about thirty minutes. When I got inside, I saw Kim before I saw Promise. She was in the kitchen fixing a sandwich.

"Wassup, Sis. Where Promise at?"

"She said she was going upstairs. I'm not getting in y'all's business, but I did tell her not to call you to come home." I looked at her, trying to figure out what was wrong. I know for a fact that it couldn't be about a bitch because I wasn't fuckin' with nobody but her and, technically, I wasn't even fuckin' her.

Nodding my head, I went up the stairs wrecking my brain, trying to figure out what Promise needed to talk about that was so important. When I made it inside the room, I didn't see her, but the bathroom door was open, and the light was on. When I walked inside, she was doing something to her face. Our eyes locked as I walked behind her and placed my hands on her waist and kissed her neck. I felt her body tense, and I backed up.

"Wassup, shorty?" I asked, never taking my eyes off of her reflection.

"So, you couldn't tell me what my father did for a living, but you can work with him? You really think what he does is okay? You don't see a problem with him trafficking human organs? Then he tells me that you're no better than him. What does that even mean?" I bunched my eyebrows together because I knew she didn't call me here because she's mad with her fuckin' pops.

"Baby, you can't be serious right now? You called me from a meeting because you finally find out what your father does, after I told you to ask him in the first place? I know that's not what I'm comprehending. If so, you sound silly as fuck trying to put that on me, shorty." I was pissed because I told that nigga to tell her, but if I knew she was going to turn that shit on me, I would've said fuck it.

"But you knew, though," she argued.

"And I told you it wasn't my place to tell you." I pointed at my chest. "I was only obligated to inform you of what I did for a living. I don't even see why you're so upset. You knew it was something illegal if he never told you. Hell, you're acting like this over some fuckin' organs when I transport drugs inside of dead bodies? You don't approve of that shit either? You hate that I use corpses as mules then burn their bodies? Newsflash shorty, this is the life that you signed up for. This ain't TV or one of those urban fiction books where everything is made up. This is real fuckin' life. *My* fuckin' reality, and now yours." I stood in front of her as she stared blankly at me. I didn't know what she wanted me to say, but I was never carrying the sins of another man. I had enough of my fuckin' own to carry around. She still didn't say anything, so I left her standing right there and went downstairs into my man cave. I didn't see Kim, but I knew she was around somewhere. When I got there, I went straight to the bar and poured a drink. This was the only thing I hated about relationships...the stupid ass arguments. That shit was bogus, and I could do without that part.

I sat in my recliner and sipped on my drink as I watched reruns of *The First 48*. In the middle of the episode, Knight called.

"Yeah?" I answered.

"Everything straight?" he asked.

"Man," I dragged out. "You know that girl called me home because she finally found out what her pops did for a living. The fuck that got to do wit' me? I told her ass from the beginning that what he did wasn't my place to tell her or my fuckin' business. I swear on Ma when I see that old ass nigga I'm punching him dead in his fuckin' mouth for bringing that shit in my fuckin' house and having the nerve to tell her he's no better than me. Nigga, get the fuck off my dick and own up to your shit." I was pissed. I really wanted to shoot his ass, but that was her father and I know it wouldn't be no coming back from that.

"Damn, Sis tripping. Aye, work out ya shit. I can handle this shit over here."

"Yeah. I might swing through later, though. I need to calm my damn nerves first." I heard my door opening and turned my head to see Promise sauntering in the room.

"I'ma call you back," I announced and hung up. I didn't say anything when she stood in front of me. I just looked at her. She was looking sexy as hell, but that wasn't going to overshadow the fact that she pissed me off.

"I'm sorry," she apologized.

When she spoke, I looked into her face and realized she had been crying. That fucked me up and had me ready to apologize for shit I didn't do.

"Come here, shorty." I reached out and grabbed her arm and pulled her into my lap.

"Why you crying?" I asked, wiping her tears away.

"I...I didn't mean to go off on you like that. It's just that I always held my father on a pedestal and with everything going on with the trafficking of all these women and children, I just lost it." She continued to cry, and I kissed her tears away.

"Baby, listen to me. I'm not into no sick shit like that. Neither are my people. If that was what your pops did, I would've told him to suck my dick. I got a mama and sister. Ain't no way in hell I could be a part of no shit like that. If it makes you feel any better, most of the people die of natural causes. Most of them come from hospitals and nursing homes and are organ donors. You know donor lists are a mile long, so if the price is right, you can get a heart or kidney without the wait. Is it unethical? Hell yeah, but so is dealing drugs and killing muthafuckas, but that's what this life entails, baby. Ain't shit sweet over here...but you." My last comment caused her to blush.

"I guess you're right. I just wasn't expecting it to be no shit like that. I'm sorry for blaming you."

"What if I'm not ready to forgive you?"

"What do I have to do to change your mind?"

"It's no fun if I got to tell you, shorty." She looked at me for a few minutes before she got off my lap and slid to her knees. I was thanking God that I wore jogging pants today because I didn't need anything to get in the way of her apologizing how she saw fit. As soon as she touched my dick, it jumped in her hands in anticipation of what was to come next.

"Sss...shit," I moaned when she sucked the head into her mouth. I leaned my head back on the headrest as I enjoyed the warmth of her mouth and the apology she was delivering.

"Fuck, baby. Just like that," I coached. She wasn't a pro yet, but with a little encouraging, she definitely got the job done and I wasn't even mad. Right when my toes started to curl, my phone started to ring. She tried getting up, but I held her head still.

"Fuck that phone. Keep going," I coached.

The ringing stopped but started right back and was pissing me the fuck off.

"What!" I snapped into the phone.

"Get to The Valley." I heard the urgency in Knight's voice and knew right away that something was wrong.

"Shit. I'm on my way." Promise removed her mouth from me when she heard me say that.

"Fuck! I got to go. Some shit must've happened because

Knight sounded urgent. I don't know how long I'm going to be, so you don't have to stay up."

"It's okay." I kissed her lips before going to the bathroom that was in here to clean my dick off and head out. Whatever this shit was, better be fuckin' important to interrupt my fuckin' nut.

———

I pulled in the back of the house in The Valley like Knight advised and pulled up beside his truck. When I got closer, I noticed that Eric, one of our drivers, was dead, and the truck was empty.

"You got to be fuckin' kidding me! Where the fuck were the rest of you niggas when this shit was happening?" I growled. "Where the fuck were you?" I was talking to his partner, OJ.

"I was opening the back door. I went to go get the shit to unload with, and when I came out, I saw a muthafucka dressed in black running into a black car. It was a bitch driving, but it was for sure a dude. I didn't notice E was dead until I stopped shooting and turned around." I listened to his explanation, and I knew it was Wood's ass. The bitch could've been his baby mama or any bitch for that matter.

"Fuck! Get this nigga inside and call his people," I ordered. I watched as he grabbed up his homeboy and took him inside like I instructed.

"You still got somebody on that nigga's house?" I asked Knight.

"Yeah. I called the nigga, and he said nobody has been there. He's been inside waiting," he informed.

"I don't need this bullshit right now."

"What you want me to do about that nigga, OJ?" he asked.

"Throw that nigga in the incinerator. It's obvious he can't do his fuckin' job. Call a meeting in the morning so we can get to the bottom of this shit."

"Bet."

I was pissed. I had to stay out this muthafucka longer than I expected, so I knew Promise would be sleeping when I got home. This nigga Wood was a pain in my fuckin' nuts. I couldn't wait to send his ass straight to hell when I laid my eyes on him.

KNASIM NINETEEN

I t was after midnight when I made it back home. Everything was dark inside, outside of the lamp in the foyer and the light above the kitchen stove. It smelled like cooked food in there, so after looking, I found a plate in the microwave with ribs, mashed potatoes, and fresh green beans on a plate. As soon as I took my shower, I was coming back down to smash that shit. After doing a check of downstairs, I trekked to the bedroom that I shared with Promise and got the surprise of my life when I walked in. The room was dim, minus the candles that she had lit throughout the room, and the only sounds that could be heard were from the music playing in the background. What set it off was Promise lying on the bed in a sheer black one-piece bodysuit that left nothing to the imagination. I didn't even need to ask what she was doing because it was clear. Without saying any words, I walked over to her and kissed her with all the passion I could muster up.

"You sure you want to do this? I know you said you wanted to wait until we got married and I've waited this long. A lil' longer won't hurt."

"I want to do this. If we're going to do this, I want to go ahead and solidify our relationship. I want you to make me yours...fully." Hearing her say that she was willingly submitting to me and only me had me swallowing the lump that formed in my throat. That was the only confirmation that I needed to hear before I grabbed the front of her throat and kissed her roughly, yet passionately at the same time.

"Baby, this is one hell of a visual, but I need you to go ahead and take that off for me." I backed up to give her room to take that little shit off. While she did that, I discarded everything I had on, and got into the bed, hovering over her. I saw the anxiety brewing in her eyes along with the love. It was crazy how I was dead set on this shit. Now I was willing to eliminate any and everything that tried to come in between us. Dipping my head, I sucked her bottom lip into my mouth and nipped it lightly before pushing my tongue through to intertwine with hers.

"Mmm," she moaned into my mouth, making my dick jump against her stomach. The feel of her small hands caressing the back of my head was sending sparks all through my body. After having enough of her sweet mouth, I trailed my kisses to her ears, chin, and neck. When I got to her neck, I bit into it before sucking on the same spot.

"Baby," she moaned.

"Hmm?" I moaned with her pierced chocolate nipple tucked between my teeth, and the other one between my thumb and index finger. No words were spoken, so I continued my assault and trailed my tongue down her stomach and over her belly button. When I got to her smooth and juicy center, I took a deep breath and basked in the scent of her. I bit the inside of her thighs that were already wet from her juices, already leaking out of her. Not wanting to deny myself any longer, I swiped my over her slick slit and her back involuntarily rose off the bed and she sucked in a deep breath.

"Ughn," she whimpered as I attacked my lips onto her hardened clit. The way I was eating her pussy should've been a crime. I wanted to make sure she was good and relaxed when I introduced this dick into her life. The way I was working my tongue and moving my head, you would've thought that I was related to that Tasmanian Devil muthafucka.

"Kna...baby...ooh shit," she whimpered as she came for the third time. I felt like that was good enough, so I sat up licked my lips clean off her juices. The way she looked at me with hooded eyes and pure adoration in her eyes had me ready to risk everything. I positioned myself on top of her, careful not to put all my weight on her in the process. I had my dick lined up perfectly with her opening and I felt her tense up.

"I need you to relax, baby," I coached. I kissed all over her face before engaging in a deep kiss I used as a distraction to push inside of her.

"Ahh," she cried out.

"It's okay, baby. You're doing good. Just let daddy get all the way in. Can you do that? Can you let daddy in?" I talked to her as a distraction as I pushed deeper inside her.

"Fuck," I groaned as she sucked me in and clawed at the back of my neck. I was only halfway in and if I was being honest, I was scared to put the rest in for the fear of nutting as soon as I did. My baby's shit felt just that good.

I worked my hips to move in and out of her so she could get adjusted to my size. I looked down into her pretty ass face as it balled up with a mixture of and pain. I felt her walls tighten around me and I had to close my eyes at the feeling. She was about to cum, and that was about to make me do the same. Pulling out of her, I dove back into her sweetness and sucked the orgasm right out of her ass.

"Knasiiim," she moaned as she rode the wave of euphoria I knew her body was currently experiencing.

While she was riding her wave, I took that as an opportunity to dive back in and this time all the way.

"Ahh!"

"Damn," we both called out when I reached the bottom. I was stuck. If I wasn't already set to marry this girl, I was damn sure going to after this. It took me a few minutes to catch my bearings, slowly stroke her center.

"You're doing good, baby," I praised. I kissed her softly as I continued to take her through a range of emotions that she had never felt before. Hell, I've never felt no shit like this either, so we were experiencing all this for the first time together.

Her light whimpers, the candlelight, the soft music, and her nails digging into every part of my body that she could grasp at were more than enough to send me over the edge. I knew it would be a matter of time before I was experiencing an orgasm of my own.

"Hold on for me, baby." She looked at me with a confused expression, but when I started drilling into her forcefully, she knew exactly what I meant.

"OH. MY. GAWD! Baby, wait. Shit...slow down," she whined. "I can't take it."

"Yeah, you can. Look at you taking this shit for daddy.

You're doing good, baby. Shit." I felt my nut rushing to escape, and I couldn't stop it if I wanted to.

"Baby."

"Fuuck," I groaned in the crook of her neck as I coated her walls. I knew I was beating my shit, and she just started sucking me off, but nothing beat the nut from some warm, tight pussy. Especially one that's only been touched by you.

My breathing had finally regulated, and I slowly lifted my weight and pulled out of her. The movement caused the both of us to tremble. Pecking her lips a few times, I just stared and admired her for a few minutes.

"Why are you looking at me like that? Was it bad?" she asked. My brows knitted together at her question.

"Was it bad? Baby, I know you feel my dick still hard. The only reason I ain't taking you down again is because I know you're sore. Shit could never be bad. I can't even describe it, but I know bad is not a word that I would ever choose. Now come on so I can run you a bath. You need to soak, and then maybe you'll be ready for another round." I got up and scooped her up in my arms and carried her into the bathroom. I ran the tub full of water and poured some of her eucalyptus bubble bath inside and watched the suds rise. I let her get in first before I slid in behind her and pulled her into my chest.

"How you feeling?" I asked, kissing her neck.

"Broken," she laughed.

"I'm sorry, baby, but you'll get used to it. I promise it won't hurt as bad."

"So, it's going to hurt?" she asked.

"I mean, you see what I'm workin' with. It won't be as bad, and I promise I'll always make you feel good in the process." I let my hand graze the skin on her stomach as I laid my head against the wall while she laid hers on my chest. This was everything I didn't know I needed. I might need to thank my pops, after all.

———————

I woke up the next morning with Promise wrapped around my body. Flashbacks of last night invaded my thoughts and my body started reacting. Before she could process what was going on, I had slid inside of her, and I damn near nutted off contact.

"Ughn...baby," she whined as I stroked her nice and slow. I needed her to adjust to me quickly and the only way I could make that happen was to slide up in her any chance I got. Besides, we got a lot of time to make up for. I worked the both of us into a well-deserved nut to start the day off with.

"Good morning." I kissed her lips and started grinding into her.

"Uh uh. Move." She started pushing me, and I couldn't do shit but laugh.

"Aight, baby. I'ma ease up off of you. I got some things to take care of this morning, anyway." I got up and headed to the bathroom and pissed before turning on the shower and going to the sink to brush my teeth. Moments later, Promise tipped into the bathroom and sat on the toilet to relieve her bladder.

"Baby, you good?" I asked.

"I'm fine, Knasim. It's just going to take a minute for me to get used to your size and appetite," she smiled.

"I mean...they say practice makes perfect." I smirked and

slapped her fat ass as she passed me to go to the sink to brush her teeth and do her face routine.

"Are you busy all day today?" she asked while I washed my body.

"Nah. I got a few meetings and some things to check on. I shouldn't be out late. Why? Wassup?"

"Nothing. I was just asking. Do you want me to cook tonight or are we going out?" When she asked that question, I remembered the food that she cooked last night that I never ate.

"Damn, baby. I forgot about the food you cooked last night. I'll eat it before I go."

"If it's been in the microwave all night, it's probably not any good."

I stepped out of the shower and reached for the towel that she handed me.

"I didn't mean to leave it out like that. I had every intention of going back downstairs to eat, but when I saw the vibe you were on last night, I said fuck that food." We shared a laugh.

"It's okay. I'm glad you liked my surprise."

"I loved that shit. That might be the way I want you to greet me from now on after a long day. When your friend leaves, you can meet me at the door just like that." I dipped my head and kissed her lips before she moved, causing a chuckle to rumble through my body.

"I'm not about to bother you. I got to get out of here, so I can make it back." I kissed her lips one more time before I left her inside the bathroom to take her shower while I got dressed. Forty-five minutes later, I was dressed and ready to go. After listening to Kim joke with Promise about last night, I kissed my girl and headed to my first meeting of the day.

My first stop was to go holla at my pops about this shit with Thad's bitch ass. I couldn't wait until I laid eyes on him again. When I walked into the building and into my father's office, I knew I didn't have to wait long. Thaddeus was sitting in front of my father's desk like everything was all good. He stood to shake my hand, and I rocked him dead in his shit.

"Knasim!" my father yelled my name, but I ignored his ass. I was waiting to see if this nigga wanted to get buck or not.

"The fuck is wrong with you?" He questioned through his blood-soaked lips.

"That's for your bullshit trickling into my fuckin' house. I told you to tell Promise what the fuck you had going on and you didn't do that shit. Now, you got her questioning me and shit. Make that the last time that shit happens, because if it does, the next hit gon' be attached to a slug." I mugged his ass and dared her said some shit.

"Son, calm down. That's what we were just talking about. We have an understanding that nothing like that will ever happen again."

"It better fuckin' not." I warned.

"Now, have you got your other situation taken care of yet?" he asked.

"Nah, I haven't. That shit got to wait, though."

"Why is that?"

"Because I'm taking Promise to Jamaica so we can get married. And before you ask, it has nothing to do with your bullshit ass rules or deadline. We actually fell in love, and I want to go ahead and marry her before shit gets too hectic." I looked at Thad, who was still nursing his lip with a mug on his face. "I haven't mentioned it to her either, so don't you go running your fuckin' mouth. Let her tell you if she chooses."

"Well, son. I'm proud of you. I knew this would work out for the better good," my father said.

"No, you didn't, but it's cool. It worked out. I'll get wit' you and Ma on the details after I get it situated. After the incident at the engagement party, I feel as if this is best." He nodded.

"I agree. Let me and your mother know what you want us or need us to do, and you know we got you," he stated. I nodded and left his office, but not before mugging Thad once more.

On the way to meet my brother, I called up Denver.

"Nigga, you call my girl more than I do," Trig fussed through the phone.

"That sounds like you slacking then," I joked. "Where Denver at? I'on want to talk to yo' ass."

"She can hear you," he said.

"Damn, nigga. You screening her calls?"

"I might be. Now talk."

"Hey, Knas. Wassup?" Denver spoke.

"Aye, Denver. You know I got you if you need help with that nigga."

"I'll remember but ain't nobody scared of Kyandri."

"So, I need you to look for a house in Jamaica for next weekend big enough to accommodate the crew."

"We going on vacation?" she asked.

"Something like that. I'm going to marry Promise while we're out there. I need to do that shit like yesterday. This shit about to get reckless and I want to make sure she's my wife to give her some kind of assurance that I'll come back. You know what I mean?"

"I do. I'll send you the information later today," she said.

"'Preciate that, Dee. Nigga, I know you still listening. Ain't you supposed to be on the way to The Bay? The fuck you in Denver's face for?"

"You worrying about the wrong shit. I'll probably beat you there," he said. I hung up in that nigga's face because he would sit and go back and forth like a bitch. I'll save that shit for Denver because I wasn't about to do it.

When I pulled up to the house in The Bay, Trig wasn't there yet. He'd just have to catch up. I was coming to say what I had to say and take my ass back home to my girl. Knight and Murda were sitting around, passing a blunt back and forth between the two of them, when I walked in.

"Not this late ass nigga being on time," Murda joked.

"Fuck you, nigga. I got shit to do, and it doesn't involve fuckin' 'round wit' you niggas all fuckin' day."

"You real sassy," Knight mentioned.

"Nigga what? Who the fuck you callin' sassy?" I snapped.

"Yo' bitch ass." Trig walked in the room talking shit as usual.

"Shut the fuck up. Now that this slow ass nigga here, let's get this shit over with."

We held our meeting about the fate of this nigga Wood. I told them we're going to let the shit die down because that way, he'll think shit sweet. That'll give us time to see if we can find out the bitch that was in that car with him that night. If we find her, we can definitely find that nigga.

"Aight, now that we got that out of the way. I got Denver

looking for a house for all of us to head to Jamaica. We need this reset and I'm going to marry Promise while we're over there. Knight and Murda. If you got to bring your women, put some muzzles on them bitches, please? I don't want no bullshit to pop off while we're out there." I loved my people, but the women those two had were advocates for doing the most, and I don't have time for the shit.

"I ain't even telling Bree's ass. Let her ass take care of her fuckin' kids for a change," he voiced.

"You trust her with the kids that long?" Trig asked.

"She ain't stupid. Unless she wants a closed casket, she'll act like she got some sense while I'm out of pocket."

"Well, I got this lil' chick I been fuckin' wit', so I'll bring her ass. It'll give me some brownie points and shit," Knight said.

"What chick?" I asked.

"You'll meet her when we get there." I nodded, praying that he didn't find himself another Teyana. After dapping everybody up, I left and headed back home. It was crazy that I was ready to get back to my girl.

"What y'all in here gossiping about?" I asked. I found them in the back, sitting on the patio. Kim was smoking, and I didn't mind at all. Like I said, that was her shit.

"We're not gossiping. How was your day?" Promise asked, kissing my lips.

"It was straight. Check it, though. We're going to Jamaica next weekend and while we're there, we're going to get married. You cool with that?" The look she gave me was one I couldn't read, but I was praying it was one that wouldn't piss me off.

"You already made plans?" she asked.

"Denver is taking care of everything. She's supposed to be getting back with me later today."

"Bitch, what you over there thinking about? This man just said he was taking you to Jamaica to get married and you're sitting there on mute. What's wrong wit' you?" Kim fussed.

"Could you hush, please? I was just over here thinking about what I was going to wear when I married the love of my life." She smiled and my heart swelled in my chest. The love I felt for this girl was ridiculous, but I wasn't complaining one bit.

"Aye, Kim. We'll be back. As a matter of fact, if you want to go out, all the keys are in the kitchen by the garage door. You can drive anything but my Lamborghini."

"Okay then. Y'all ain't got to tell me twice. I'm gone."

Shit, she could drive that muthafucka too, if she wanted. The only thing I was concerned about at this moment was my girl and what she possessed between her legs.

PROMISE

Twenty

When Knasim came home and said he wanted to go to Jamaica and get married, I was floored. I never expected him to want to do it so soon after we technically just got engaged. When he told me the reasoning, I was a little apprehensive at first but after he broke it down to me; I understood where he was coming from and agreed. Kim took full advantage of leaving the house and Knasim took full advantage of it and fucked me all over every inch of it. She didn't come back until the next morning and when she told me where she was and with who, I almost passed the fuck out.

"You did what with who?" I damn near yelled.

"Bitch, quiet down. You heard me. I went to the club, and I saw Kyan there. We started talking, and he told me what he's been going through with his wife. It wasn't my business, but it felt like he needed to vent, so I listened. We went to his suite, and I let him run everything down to me. After countless blunts and shots, one thing led to another, and that nigga had me on my knees with my face pressed into the mattress. I thought it would be weird when we woke up, but it wasn't. We exchanged numbers, and he said he'll hit me up later today." By the time she was finished, my damn face was on the floor.

"Bitch, did you like it?" she whispered.

"Did she like what?" Knasim crept up and asked.

"Uhm," I started to lie.

"Promise don't even lie. I already talked to Murda, and that ain't none of my business. All I'm going to say is, watch out for yourself, Kim. Baby, I got to make a run. I'll be gone for a few hours." He kissed me and left me and Kim in the kitchen as he left through the garage door.

"Well, I'm not even going to judge you. Anybody with eyes can see it's something going on with him and Aubree. Just be careful," I warned her.

"I am, friend. I'm just having a little fun while I'm here. Now, let's go shopping so we can be ready for Jamaica." That was music to my ears. I texted Denver and Knicole in the group chat that we created and let them know the plans so they could meet us. To think I didn't even want to come to Wood Haven, but I'm glad my father convinced me to do so. I now had new friends and a man that was forced upon me, but loves me like our love story started conventionally. I wouldn't trade any of this for anything in this world or the next.

———

"So, Promise. Are you ready to marry my brother? I mean you done been fast and gave up your coochie already. We were supposed to have a pact, and you broke it, heifer." Knicole rolled her eyes as she spoke.

"A pact?" Denver asked.

"Yeah. A virginity pact, but this bitch let Knas talk her out of her draws. I knew she was going to do it."

"And how did you figure that?" I asked.

"I told you; I had friends that dated my brothers. Them nigga's could make a nun backslide." We shared a laugh as we sipped our drinks at the restaurant Knasim took me on our first date.

"Those Richmond's know they can be some charmers," Denver said, and I so-signed. I looked at Kim slyly, or at least I thought I did.

"Uh uh. What was that look about?" Knicole asked. "You hunching on my other brother?" she asked.

"No, I'm not hunching on Knight," Kim said.

"Well, who is it because I like you and all, but I know you ain't sleep with Kyandri and laughing in Denver's face?" Knicole had her face balled up like she smelled something funky.

"Now, why would I do that to Denver?" Kim asked. When she said that, it was like a light switch went off in Denver's head.

"You and Kyan?" Denver whispered. The look on Kim's face said it all.

"What the hell?" Knicole yelled. "Girl, I want to say so many things right now, but I'm not. We all know Kyan and there definitely had to be a good reason behind it, and I want to know what it is."

We all sat around and listened as Kim recalled the events

that happened between her and Kyan last night. I wanted to feel some kind of way about him being married, but Knicole and Denver confirmed what he had told Kim. Hell, I had no room to talk because my fiancé was a complete stranger when I met him. If Kim was the one to help him cope, then so be it.

————

I had been to Jamaica a once before, but I don't remember it being this pretty. We decided not to bring our parents because this was a trip for us as well as our wedding and we didn't need them in the way. Besides, I didn't want to be around my father right now.

"Baby, you like it?" Knasim asked from behind me.

"I do. It's so pretty out here. Look at that water."

"It ain't got shit on you though," he flirted.

"You always know what to say, huh?"

"Damn right. You ready to be my wife?"

"Damn right," I mocked him.

We were set to get married tomorrow night, and I was both nervous and excited at the same time. We were all going out tonight to celebrate. You could tell the guys were close like I was with the girls, because none of them seemed surprised about how cozy Kim and Kyan were. I guess they said they were both consenting adults that could make decisions for themselves. We ended up going to a nice restaurant before heading to a strip club. It wouldn't be normal if the guys didn't secure a section for us to turn up in. We ended up inviting some strippers up and making it a bachelor/bachelorette celebration.

"Aye! Promise don't let her show you up in front yo' nigga.

Show 'em how we do it back at The Cannon!" Kim cheered me on as the stripper took my hand and had me get up and dance with her.

"Chy, you gon' get pregnant tonight watch," Denver said.

"I ain't babysitting either," Knicole, co-signed.

"I bet you will. I had to babysit yo' bratty ass," Knasim said as he pulled me in his lap."

"You bringing up old stuff." She waved him off.

"I'm gon' fuck you real good tonight, so I hope you ready?" His words had me clenching my thighs together.

"I thought we said we weren't going to have sex anymore until after we're married?"

"You said that bullshit. Not me. I waited two damn months. The fuckin' wait is over." I would be lying if I said I was mad because I damn sure wasn't. I was fully prepared to let him do whatever he wanted to do with me, and he did just that when we got back to our room.

———

The time was finally here. I was about to marry the man I didn't even know I needed. It was so much drama in the beginning that I didn't think I would last thirty days. Knasim proved me wrong because he was nothing like I pegged him to be. He was so sweet and caring with me. That warranted him to have all of me for the rest of our lives. While I stood under the gazebo and stared into his eyes as he recited his vows that I didn't even know he prepared.

"Promise, when I ran into in the boutique, I knew then you

were someone I wanted to have in my life. Who not that are families were already in cahoots?" He laughed. "Shit was nostalgic to say the least that you were in my parent's kitchen not even checking for me. People probably think it was our families that got us together, but I knew it was felt. I felt it the first time I laid my eyes on you. Something stirred inside me that I never felt before. That's why this shit was so easy for me. You were made for me, and I promise you that I'll show you every day just how much you mean to a nigga like me." I couldn't even say anything if I wanted to because his words had me choked up. He kissed my lips as he wiped the tears that were falling from my eyes. When the preacher announced us husband and wife, he wore a huge grin on his face that mimicked mine as he kissed me as our friends cheered.

"How you feeling, Mrs. Richmond?" he asked as we shared our first dance as husband and wife.

"I feel like I'm floating and don't want to come down from," I admitted.

"Good, because I don't plan on letting you come down." We shared a kiss until Knight came and interrupted us.

"Aye, bruh. I know this your wedding night and shit, but they got eyes on Wood's baby mama." I listened to what they were saying. I knew of the situation because Knasim said he didn't want to keep me out of anything.

"Handle that, while I enjoy my wife," he said, and Knight nodded. He walked off, calling Kyan, and they went off to the side to talk. Knasim was still staring at me, and it caused my face to flush.

"Are you happy?" He asked me.

"I am." I smiled.

"Good, because you in this shit for life."

Welcome to The RCF!!!

Thank y'all for reading the first book from The Richmond Family Saga. There will be four standalones in total, with a collective book at the end. Each book will highlight each character's story while the others are showcased in the background. Also, each book will pick up where the other left off...some may overlap. So if you think something was left open, it was on purpose, because it will be showcased in the future books. The order will be Knasim, Knight, Kyandri, then Kyan before the collective book. I love these characters already and I hope you enjoy them just as much as I do. Enjoy Knasim's story and WELOCME TO THE RCF!!!!

DOPE BOOKS BY TACARRA

*Forever By His Side: Jahkel & Yamari https://amzn.to/3YzvaR2
*A Street King Got Me In My Feelings https://amzn.to/3SFzcoK
*Baecation https://a.co/d/cDWQlpP
*Candy Reign https://a.co/d/dflb4yA
*Without You I Have Nothing To Lose https://amzn.to/3E4OL4l

KEEP IN TOUCH

*Facebook Page https://bit.ly/2LO5KO8
*Facebook Group https://bit.ly/37wB6Rn
*Instagram https://bit.ly/3lZCAG0
*Twitter: https://bit.ly/3jVKw08
*TikTok http://bit.ly/34GvxlB
*Threads https://bit.ly/2OTm1QT
*Amazon Author Page https://amzn.to/39GO1TE
*Mailing List https://bit.ly/3NT7Wjw

Made in the USA
Monee, IL
11 April 2025

15614368R00115